Advance praise for
This Must Be the Place

"The place in *This Must Be the Place* is Merdale, a college town fastened to the Kansas prairie. Susan Jackson Rodgers depicts it so vividly I felt I had been transported there to live again through the summer of 1983. If only I could have handled the Reagan era with as much spunk and intelligence as Rodgers's heroine, Thea Knox. I can't remember when I last met a character as smart and open to the world as Thea. This book is a treat from beginning to end."

—Elizabeth Stuckey-French,
author of *The Revenge of the Radioactive Lady*

"This well-written novel introduced me to a place and set of characters that felt fresh, interesting, and entertaining. I enjoyed immersing myself in the unexpected community of Merdale."

—Caitlin Horrocks,
author of *This Is Not Your City*

"Susan Jackson Rodgers has created an utterly winsome narrator in Thea, plucky, observant, and honest. She's the best guide we could hope for on this journey through the Land of Oz, better known as contemporary America. Rodgers writes with sublime detail and fearless energy—every page crackles with humor, compassion, and derring-do. Thea has enough courage for all of us as she travels cross country, picking up a stray dog who becomes her familiar, and begins to unwind the complicated memories of her past when she arrives at Aunt Wendy's house. This is a must-read for anyone who has wondered how to make sense of the chaos of the current times amidst the unresolved questions of a past that seems blown to pieces by storm winds. What is love? Who are the people who claim to be our parents? How am I to enter the ordinary world after coming back from Oz? Rodgers creates an original cast of characters who are so alive that we believe they must be real people, we come to care so much about them. This is a novel to be read late into the night and then shared with friends and relatives—you'll see what I mean!"

—Jonis Agee,
author of *The Bones of Paradise*
and *The River Wife*

"One of the strengths of *This Must Be the Place* is the carefully constructed voice of the narrator. Engaging and vulnerable, it made me want to go along on this journey with her."

—John McNally,
author of *After the Workshop*

"This tough-talking novel beguiles the reader with its forthright sexuality, its prickly characters, and its surprising representation of the Midwest. Many show-stopping paragraphs and a twister of a plot! I was delighted to spend time with Susan Jackson Rodgers, who exudes passion, poetry, humor, hard-won wisdom, resilience, and grit."

—Trudy Lewis,
author of *The Empire Rolls*

THIS MUST BE THE PLACE

THIS MUST BE THE PLACE

SUSAN JACKSON RODGERS

SWITCHGRASS BOOKS
NORTHERN ILLINOIS UNIVERSITY PRESS   DeKalb IL

Published by Switchgrass Books, an imprint of Northern Illinois University Press
Northern Illinois University Press, DeKalb 60115
© 2017 by Northern Illinois University Press
All rights reserved
Printed in the United States of America
26 25 24 23 22 21 20 19 18 17   1 2 3 4 5
978-0-87580-768-3 (paper)
978-1-60909-227-6 (e-book)
Book and cover design by Yuni Dorr
Cover photo by Aubrey Carroll

Lyrics from "This Must Be the Place (Naive Melody)," words and music by David Byrne, Chris Frantz, Jerry Harrison, and Tina Weymouth, used by permission of Alfred Music, © 1983 WB Music Corp. and Index Music, Inc. All rights administered by WB Music Corp. All rights reserved.

Lyrics from "Burning Down the House," lyrics by David Byrne and music by David Byrne, Chris Frantz, Jerry Harrison, and Tina Weymouth, used by permission of Alfred Music, © 1983 WB Music Corp. and Index Music, Inc. All rights administered by WB Music Corp. All rights reserved.

Library of Congress Cataloging-in-Publication Data
Names: Rodgers, Susan Jackson, 1960– author.
Title: This must be the place : a novel / Susan Rodgers.
Description: DeKalb, IL : Northern Illinois University Press, 2017
Identifiers: LCCN 2017019906 (print) | LCCN 2017023961 (ebook) | ISBN 9781609092276 (ebook) | ISBN 9780875807683 (paperback) | ISBN 9781609092276 (e-book)
Subjects: | BISAC: FICTION / Literary. | GSAFD: Bildungsromans.
Classification: LCC PS3618.O356 (ebook) | LCC PS3618.O356 T48 2017 (print) | DDC 813/.6—dc23
LC record available at https://lccn.loc.gov/2017019906

FOR SAMUEL, MARGARET, AND BENJAMIN—
MY FAVORITE KANSANS

PART I

"If we walk far enough," said Dorothy,
"we shall sometime come to someplace, I am sure."
—L. Frank Baum, *The Wonderful Wizard of Oz*

FOREST, TREES

WHEN I WAS TWENTY-TWO, I cut off my hair in Lovelock, Nevada. I'd been driving with the boom box blaring and the windows down, so when I got sick of my hair lashing at my face, I stopped at the Two Stiffs Selling Gas Mini Mart and borrowed a pair of scissors from the cowboy clerk. He didn't ask what I needed them for, just pointed me to the bathroom "around back," where I wrapped my thick ponytail around my wrist and started sawing. If you've never taken scissors to your own head, then you're unfamiliar with the combination of horror and exhilaration that ensues. Widows and nuns are shorn, like sheep. I ignored the implications.

I set the ponytail ceremoniously on the paper towel dispenser and stared into the blurry mirror, the metal kind they have at highway rest stops, then clipped at the remaining hair in angry snips as if to say, "I'll show you!" I wasn't sure who the "you" was. Maybe I was the you. Or maybe the you was my best friend, Emily, heading to Micronesia for a year, then law school. (Dearest Em, always with the perfect plan.) Or maybe it was our landlord back in Santa Cruz, or Emily's brother Eddie. Or my parents, who'd sold our house—*sold* it—which wouldn't have been so terrible, except that I'd planned to live there for the summer. They announced their news three days before my departure. The Hudson Valley was a seller's market, Mom explained. She and Dad just wanted to put out feelers, the offer exceeded the asking price, *it all happened so fast.* Yes. Yes it did. Just because you get an offer doesn't mean you have to take it, I wanted to say, but didn't bother. There was no reasoning with those people. They invited me to join them for the summer—they'd bought an RV, utterly out of character—but we all knew what a bad idea that was.

I was heading back east anyway, because *my* plan, my original plan, the plan that had included house-sitting before there was no house to sit, was to deliver Emily's Buick Skylark to Eddie. The situation with Eddie had recently become ... problematic. I resolved not to think about him until I got there.

I did my best to sweep up the hair with paper towels, then scrubbed my hands with powdery soap and shook out my shirt. Back in the store, the poker-faced cowboy barely registered my new look, or the ponytail I carried like a trophy. He had seen it all before, or he had seen nothing. Either way, it didn't matter. I handed him the scissors. He wore a pearl-button plaid shirt, Stetson hat, Wrangler jeans, and a belt with a big horseshoe buckle. "Straight out of central casting," my father would say.

"You're leaking oil."

I looked down at my cutoffs, as if he meant me. He smiled and gestured toward the Buick.

"I figured that's what that was," I said. The truth is, I hadn't noticed the dark stain under the car. I walked through the store, selecting refreshments. He thwacked a pack of cigarettes against the counter then lit one—those were the days when everyone still smoked inside—exhaling out of the corner of his mouth. "Where you headed?"

"New York?"

"You're asking me?"

He was cute, this Marlboro Man, or son of the Marlboro Man. He was probably my age, though a childhood spent in the desert sun had left its mark. I imagined a quickie in the storage room, the "Back in ten minutes" sign on the door. I didn't willfully imagine it, I'm not (always) that kind of girl—the image just popped into my mind: the unbuckled buckle, hat pushed back on his head, and me bent over a carton of soda fountain cups. I blushed, as if he were privy to these thoughts.

He walked bowlegged to the automotive section, next to a slot machine, and returned with four cans of Pennzoil. "You should get it fixed in Salt Lake. In the meantime, add oil as you go." He bagged my purchases—the oil, two Cokes, butter rum Life Savers, a bag of corn nuts, and a *People* magazine. "Princess Leia Helps Destroy the Empire in *Jedi*." "A Tornado

Named Debra Winger Has a Whirl with Nebraska's Governor." I noticed the cowboy's shiny wedding ring.

"Newlywed?" I asked.

"Yep. But we've been dating since the eighth grade."

"Well, then, it's time you made an honest woman of her."

He smiled. "I'll give you a hand with that oil."

"I won't say no." I dropped the ponytail into the bag.

We walked outside into the wall of heat. I dreaded getting back into the car. The trip had sounded like a big adventure when Emily and I hatched the scheme back in March, but I'd only left California that morning and I was already tired and bored and sweaty, and now on top of everything else I had this haircut. The cowboy released the hood, propped it open, and unscrewed the cap on the oil thingy. I didn't bother pretending I knew where anything was. I wondered where he'd taken his child bride for their honeymoon. Lake Tahoe? Vegas? "Is she pregnant?" The words were out before I could stop them, but he didn't flinch.

"Four months." He dropped the hood shut and wiped his hands on a bandana he pulled from his back pocket, like a magician. I put my hand out to thank him. He looked down at it as if he had never shaken a woman's hand before, and maybe he hadn't, maybe women in Lovelock didn't shake hands when they were introduced to people. But he shook it anyway, with a wry smile. I really hope that wife of yours has a sense of humor, I thought.

"You be careful," he said.

"It's probably too late for that."

He touched the brim of his hat, as if in agreement.

~

I stopped for lemon meringue pie at a Winnemucca diner. I'd eaten a slice of cherry in Truckee and decided to conduct a national pie survey. The paper place mat listed Fun Facts: Winnemucca, City of the Paved Streets, proud home of the Buckaroo Hall of Fame and a bank that Butch Cassidy robbed back in 1900, as well as—the waitress told me with a wink—the oldest brothel in Nevada. Average rainfall: 8 inches per year. Population: 5,303. The pie? Tender crust, but the meringue was weepy. I gave it a B.

On the way out of town I passed a couple of casinos, a discount liquor store, and three hotels, all with flickering No Vacancy signs. Maybe there was a special that week at the brothel. Buy one, get one free! I turned up the music. *Hold tight*, the song warned. *We're in for nasty weather*. But no, the western sky was a vast deep blue fading to lighter blue at the horizon, and not a cloud in sight. In Hollywood they used to paint skies on backdrops because the real one looked fake, just as this one did.

I headed toward Elko, where I'd stop for the night. Along the way I inventoried the landscape. Flat open land, sagebrush dotting stark brown mountains, railroad tracks, an old church with a steeple, a barbed wire fence in a line from here to the ends of the earth. Nothing but stretches of nothing. I tried to quell a rising panic, but my options looked similarly bleak. I couldn't go back to California. Danny, the cute landlord, had rented our apartment to another pair of pretty college girls. He'd no doubt already selected the one he could count on for the occasional rendezvous. And anyway, Eddie was waiting for me. He had this idea about us. The last time we'd talked—I cringed thinking about it. But I couldn't just *not* show up. Emily once said, "The trouble with you, Dorothea, is that you can't see the forest *or* the trees." We'd laughed at that, but it didn't seem so hilarious now.

I'd just have to wait and see what happened. I'd figure out the next step as I went along. My specialty! The next step could be anything. Back then, though, it usually involved a boy. A California surfer with time on his hands. A cowboy, showing me where to put the Pennzoil. A backpacker crossing a street in Cheyenne.

Or a golden-haired man, standing in a field, hoe in hand, beckoning. Yes, that one. *Jimmy*. He was looking for me, too.

I don't know how he would tell the story of that summer. Or any of the other people I met—Nick, George, or even Amira whose life I effectively ruined, though she had it out for me, too. It's funny though, of all the people I knew back then, it's Amira I wonder about the most. Jimmy's the one I *think* about, the one whose voice still comes back to me, whose jokes I still laugh at, whose face I still hold dear. But Amira, she's the mystery. I've searched the Internet for clues, but nothing comes up. It's as if she really did just disappear.

When Emily and I said good-bye, she gave me ten envelopes already stamped and addressed to Yap Island. "Write to me," she said. "I can't wait to see how it all turns out." "Me either," I said. But in fact it took me a long time to write that first letter. It was as if I had fallen into someone else's story and couldn't reach back far enough to touch my old life. I wasn't dreaming, but I wasn't quite awake either.

∼

I made my way through Salt Lake City (peach pie, crumble topping, A-), Cheyenne (goopy blueberry, C+), and then drove another hundred years to Kearney, Nebraska (key lime, impeccable balance of tart and sweet, a solid A). In Grand Island I splurged on a room at the Best Western. I'd planned a side trip to Merdale, Kansas, to visit my aunt Wendy, so the next night's lodging would be free. Wendy was my mother's half sister, but she was only ten years older than me and not very auntlike. The timing turned out to be fortuitous—the oil situation was getting worse.

The morning I left for Merdale I had breakfast (banana cream, B+) at a Perkins Restaurant in Grand Island, where, my chatty seatmate at the counter informed me, it was the anniversary of the Night of the Twisters. "Seven tornadoes, all touched down, and they didn't move in a straight line," Norma told me. She waved her cigarette around, still awed by the storm's agility and power. "They looped back over their own paths, crisscrossing themselves." The wreckage would've filled the local landfill past capacity, so the clever townspeople found a spot in a park and dug a hole six feet deep and two hundred feet wide. They filled the hole with debris and continued piling it up until they'd made a heap forty feet high. They planted grass on the pile and called it Tornado Hill. "Kids sled there in the winter," Norma said, adjusting her black wig as if it were a rakish beret.

She asked where I was headed, and when I told her, she smiled. "Merdale. Now, that's a lovely little corner of the world." She started to say something else, but then nodded toward the window. "Looks like there's a storm brewing. You should probably hit the road." I hadn't noticed the dark smudges at the edges of the sky. I bade Norma farewell and left the waitress a big tip. She'd given me crystal clear directions to the interstate and also told me I had good cheekbones, which was probably a kindhearted attempt to console me about my asylum-inmate hairdo. I'd aimed for Mia Farrow, and missed.

I stopped at a gas station convenience store (the Kum & Go—really?) where I picked up ice for my cooler, a six-pack of Diet Coke, another quart of oil, and, as luck would have it, a dog. I was putting the sodas on ice when she leaped into the car. She was a scruffy terrier with maybe some yellow Lab, small- to medium-sized. No collar, no tag. She scrambled up to the front seat and put her head on her paws and looked up at me with doleful brown eyes, et cetera et cetera. Oh yes, she knew all the doggy tricks. I scanned the parking lot, expecting someone to appear with leash in hand. No one in sight. I looked back at her. She lifted one ear. Then the wind picked up, reminding me I was in a hurry. A raindrop splatted on my forehead. The dog was in good shape, well fed, bright eyed, toenails trimmed. Back inside the store, the cashier said he'd put up Found Dog signs and checked with the shelter. "Someone dumped her a few days ago," he said. "It happens a lot. I just called Animal Control."

I thanked him and got back in the car, imagining a line of vehicles slowing down and depositing unwanted pets one after the other on the side of the road. There are people who pay thousands for fancy breeds, and there are people who pick up strays or shelter mutts and pride themselves on this practice. I was raised in the latter tribe. I consulted Wendy's directions to Merdale. She'd drawn a little map that looked like a child's treasure map, a green X marking her house. I checked the sky again. How bad could it be? Just then the dogcatcher pulled up in a white van with no windows. I looked straight ahead and pulled out of the parking lot as if I were eluding capture, but no one cared if I took that dog. She scooched closer to me, inch by inch, and put her head on my lap. Regret mode hit immediately, in spite of my noble principles. I had no business taking her on. What landlord was going to let me have a dog? Dogs were never allowed anywhere. Even Danny hadn't allowed pets. Maybe Wendy could help me find her a home. She was a good dog. "You're a good girl," I told her, and she wagged her tail slowly, as if she mostly had been told otherwise. "You *are*. You're a very good girl. What's your name, anyway?" I reeled off possibilities, trying to imagine what a treacherous hateful evil dog ditcher would pick. Something obvious, like Lady or Sandy or

Ginger. But she just sighed. I spotted the Grand Union and pulled into the parking lot. She sat up and stuck her nose out the cracked window.

I bought a bag of kibble, two bowls, a gallon of water, a collar, and a leash, a considerable dent in my budget. She drank and ate while I reeled off more options. "Liza, Lucy, Stella, Bella, Loni, Jonie." She didn't look up until I got to Josie. Joslyn, then. Josie for short. We settled back into our spots on the Buick's bench seat like old traveling companions. The barometric pressure was dropping—I could feel a thudding sensation in my head and gut. My skin felt prickly. I should've left earlier. It was stupid to drive into weather, in a car with every dashboard warning light blazing and blinking and a slack seat belt that I wore mostly for show, like a beauty pageant sash. I perseverated on the whole dog thing, how I couldn't afford a dog, how I had no place to live and my future was uncertain and getting a dog was the dumbest idea ever. Though I hadn't actually gotten a dog—she had gotten me, and who was it who said that when a dog chooses you, you have to say yes? I wasn't sure. Probably my father.

Muscular greenish-black clouds were rolling toward me. Merdale was just a few hours away. With luck I could get ahead of the storm. But by the time I reached the interstate, the rain began, followed quickly by a downpour. I mean that. A *pouring down*. Then the rain turned to hail, pea-sized at first, then grape, then, I don't know what, *chestnut*. Crazy. Would the windshield crack? Nope—back to rain, and a fierce wind.

The farther south I went, the worse the storm got. You can always see it coming, on the prairie. You know exactly what you're in for. You can see it in the rearview mirror, too. The sky is everywhere. I was used to weak flashes of light in the distance, not these vivid jagged bolts, like the kind Zeus carries around. Plus, *sheets of rain*. There they were, off in the distance—like silver shower curtains hanging from the clouds. And then they weren't distant at all, and the Buick's windshield wipers whipped from side to side, no match for the deluge. I belted out a couple of hits from *Hair*, then switched to *The Fantasticks*, hollering off-key as usual. Broadway show tunes, my family's version of hymns.

I inched along, taillights of the car ahead appearing so suddenly I was afraid I'd plow into it. It was like driving through a car wash. I tried to remember what hydroplaning was, and what you were supposed to do if hydroplaning occurred. Was it like ice, when you steer into the skid? And then almost instantly the rain subsided, and I drove into a nearly dry patch of road, as if the storm knew to stay within designated boundaries. My hands gripped the wheel, my shoulders and back ached from the effort of steering. I thought about those seven twisters.

I nearly missed Wendy's exit. When I reached the off-ramp, I crossed over one of the invisible lines. Sunrays descended in wide gold bands from wrung-out clouds. The clouds looked like the Colorforms I played with as a child, superimposed shapes on the sky, as if you could peel them off. I relaxed my grip, unhunched my shoulders. I remembered Danny's back rubs. He was just one credit short from getting his massage therapy certification. He would never finish, I knew, because he was lazy and rich. I rolled my shoulders forward and back. Josie had taken refuge in the passenger seat footwell during the worst of my singing. "Look at this," I murmured, and she hopped up next to me. The road was silver, shiny, as if made of mercury. The wet grasses on either side glittered gold and green in the watercolor light. The sky was violet. Glaciated hills rolled like ocean waves, one after the other. Then a river with cotton-wood trees clustered along its banks, the undersides of the leaves flickering, and gradually some farmhouses and pastures and fields, and the beginnings of civilization. "Merdale," a sea in a valley. "How darling," my mother would say.

The exit led straight onto Main Street, with its stagy western brick storefronts. One window displayed fanciful handblown glass objects in reds and blues and greens, another featured specialty chocolates and a rainbow of jelly beans, a third, Shasta daisies and irises and tulips in big buckets.

If memory served, Aunt Wendy had lived here since graduating from Merdale College. She and Phoebe, my mom, had different mothers, and their father wasn't enthusiastic about getting the two girls together. I'd only met Wendy once, when I was ten and she was almost twenty. During the summers my parents worked the art festival circuit and conducted workshops. My father directed plays in old barns that had been converted into theaters. Sometimes I went along, sometimes not. One summer they traveled around Greece on a fellowship, studying Sophocles or somebody. I went to Ohio, where Wendy was charged with taking care of me and her younger brother, Henry. Wendy's father—my pseudo-grand-father—worked at the Farm Bureau, and her mother was a nurse. They had recently become Quakers. Every Sunday morning people came over and sat in a circle in the living room, waiting for the spirit to move them. Then they'd say what was on their minds. I was good at drawing block letters, so the Quakers put me in charge of making posters for their antiwar vigils. Mostly, though, I lay on the floor and watched dust motes make their slow tour of the TV room where the TV had been removed because my grandfather had decided he didn't believe in it, or radio either. One afternoon, on a snooping expedition, I found *Story of O* in Grandpa's nightstand drawer. Marginalia and underlining and little sketches filled every page. After that I wasn't bored anymore, just confused.

Now Wendy lived on a street with enormous elm trees on either side that nearly touched at the top. Tidy bungalows with white trim and front porches faced each other. Wendy's house stood out: not white or gray or brown, but cornflower blue, with a lime-green porch swing and Adirondack chairs in yellow and red. Instead of a front lawn, she'd planted wildflowers and prairie grasses and replaced the sidewalk leading up to the house with a curving stone path. Garden gnomes of varying sizes stood guard. Wind chimes, six or seven of them, hung from the porch. There was a lot of activity at the birdbath, but the two cats lolling on the porch steps were unconcerned. I wondered what the neighbors thought of all this whimsy and color and clutter on their otherwise quiet, uniform street. I wanted to live there, or even next door to there.

"Stay," I told Josie through the car's open window. She watched me and the cats with terrific concentration. To think that people would take the time to train a dog, then abandon her at a Kum & Go.

The orange-striped cat had six toes on its front paws. The white one had a green eye and a blue eye. They licked my hands and purred. A light breeze stirred the wind chimes. The houses next door seemed farther away. Wendy's yard widened as I approached the porch, or else the space surrounding me had warped. I felt dizzy, as if I'd bumped my head and was just now coming to.

Wendy emerged from the blue house and into the brilliant sunshine, and she was bright and shining in her white gauzy ruffled top, arms spread to greet me. "Look at you, all grown up!" she exclaimed. She wore her dark reddish hair piled loosely on top of her head. A light dusting of freckles sprinkled across her nose like glitter. Her fuchsia shorts matched her lipstick, her only makeup. When she hugged me—she was a good head taller and at least sixty pounds heavier—she smelled like warm rocks at the beach. She managed not to say anything about my hair, but I could tell it was a struggle.

"And who is this?" she said, spotting Josie over my shoulder. Before I could answer, Wendy called out, "C'mere, sweetie," and the dog jumped out the car window and dashed up the path. They greeted each other like long-lost pals.

Wendy asked me about my drive, and the car, and the storm, and I told her about the near-hydroplaning and the lightning, and she spread her arms out again—the gesture seemed theatrical this time—and announced, "But you're here. You made it through to the other side." She smiled as if she knew something I didn't. I felt that she could see me wholly, that I had entered her world and she was in charge now.

She scooped up a cat in each arm and led me inside. The house was filled with artifacts that Wendy's boyfriend, Bob, had brought back from his travels. Buddhas and incense burners, batik wall hangings, wooden carvings.

"Bob will be home later," she said. "He's on his rounds."

"He's a doctor?" And for a split second, I thought of Eddie, Emily's brother, the soon-to-be-recipient of the Buick. Eddie was in medical school.

"Oh—no, no." She laughed. She opened the door to a small room where a dozen guitars were displayed on stands. "He *wants* to be a rock-and-roll star. But in the meantime he's a graduate student in wildlife biology. He does this rehabilitation thing with injured animals. It's all very romantic." She looked at the guitars, then shut the door. "That'll be the nursery, someday," she confided. Bob's guitars, I thought, begged to differ.

She led me down the hall. As we surveyed the guest room I could imagine a magic wand in her hand, tapping each thing into existence. Twin bed, a wicker dresser, a paper Chinese lantern over a small table that could serve as a desk. A mobile of wooden birds hung over the bed. I touched a bird to set it in motion.

"Bob made that," she said. "Now, let's have some lunch and let you rest for a bit. Then we'll do something about your hair."

~

After lunch I lay on the narrow bed and closed my eyes. I could feel myself slipping toward a dark mood, or the darkness edging toward me. I worked to get it under control. I did my breathing exercises and visualizations, and when the panic continued to rise, I took a mental tour of my old house. This is something I used to do as a sleep trick, and it always worked to calm me down. Except this time, I knew I'd never see the actual place again. I'd never step into the living room, with its leafy patterned wallpaper and antique rolltop desk and crammed bookshelves, or the sun porch, my favorite spot, where I could fall onto the welcoming couch with its shabby-genteel chintz and familiar-smelling cushions, a pleasant mustiness mixed with my father's pipe tobacco. I'd never lie on my bed surrounded by girlhood relics, displayed shrine-like as I had left them, the usual stuffed animals and books and photo booth photos pinned to a bulletin board, all efforts to mimic the bedrooms of my junior high school friends. I'd never again poke around the attic, peeking into boxes of Christmas ornaments, photo albums, board games, my mother's old dance costumes. (What had happened to all that stuff? Had Phoebe and Lyman rented a storage unit? Dumped everything at the Goodwill? I didn't want to know.) But even so. In my mind everything remained intact, and I was a wispy specter gliding through the rooms, swimming down hallways and shimmying under tables, my hands moving filmily over each chair and cabinet and rug and light switch, touching everything as if to commit it to its proper place.

By the time Wendy summoned me to the backyard, I was feeling better. She set up a barstool for my haircut. Comb, scissors, hand mirror, towel, folded sheet, and spray bottle were lined up neatly on the picnic table. She handed me a gin and tonic and draped the sheet around me. I sat down obediently. I figured she couldn't make things any worse. And I liked the way she looked at me, not with Emily's cool appraisal, but with the eyes of someone who saw the rich possibilities. She fluffed my ragged hair, lifting up the uneven sections and measuring them loosely with her fingers, cocking her head and strategizing. She told me about her advising job at the college. During the summer she worked at a greenhouse, mostly for the discount. "What I'd really like is to have a baby, but Bob 'isn't ready.'" She made a face. "I'm working on him though. I'll be thirty-two soon. I don't have forever."

A Keith Jarrett album played through the kitchen window. I felt drowsy in the sun, the spicy gin and bright taste of lime on my lips, the backyard shady and cool, the rhythmic sound of Wendy's scissors snipping, Keith's casual glissandos and weirdly erotic moans carrying us along, so that I could almost have fallen asleep again. I could've been sitting there for a week, and I wouldn't have been surprised.

"Okay," she said, rousing me, "see what you think." She held up the mirror.

She had given me the look I'd been after in that Lovelock restroom, a moment that already felt long ago. I remembered my sawed-off ponytail, which I'd stuck in the side pocket of a suitcase—I'd have to do something with it. Burn it or bury it in some ritual, to cast off my past self? Send it to Danny, ex-landlord/lover, who preferred long-haired girls? I turned my head to admire myself from each angle, exclaiming my gratitude.

"It does look good," Wendy agreed. "I'm glad you like it. And, honey, I'm glad you're here." She put her hands on my shoulders and kissed my forehead. I imagined a bright pink lipstick mark. I didn't wipe it off. I wanted it there.

～

I met Bob over veggie burgers and green beans. He was slight and slouchy, especially compared to Wendy, but somehow they went together. He was a familiar type—"redolent of cannabis," as Emily used to say. I preferred Wendy's cocktails to the joint he offered me after dinner. "No thanks." I lifted my glass.

He smiled and toasted me back with the joint. "You guys should come with me tomorrow. James is keeping the coolest owl out at his house."

"Jimmy Ward," Wendy said, as if by way of explanation.

For dessert we ate pie made with the small, sweet strawberries straight from her garden. A+, no question. We sat in the backyard watching the first fireflies of summer. Bob picked out tunes on an acoustic guitar. Wendy and I caught up on family news, since our families weren't really in touch. Her mother was a hospice nurse now. Her father had just retired and spent most of his time writing angry letters to congressmen about trickle-down economics and tax cuts and farm foreclosures. Her brother worked in HR. I didn't know what HR was, and even after she explained it to me, I wasn't sure what a person in HR would do all day. I summarized my parents' latest adventures, but omitted the part about the house. I felt embarrassed about my predicament, as if I'd left my life unattended at a bus station and returned to find it gone.

"Your parents are such a kick," Wendy said. "Phoebe and Lyman are like a gorgeous messy painting or, you know, one of those wacky avant-garde modern dance things that you don't understand but can't stop thinking about."

I agreed. "They're messy, all right."

"Life is messy, isn't it? The neat and tidy people, walking in their straight lines—they're a mess, too." She put her head back and closed her eyes. Citronella torches burned in a circle around us to ward off mosquitoes. Wendy's face was luminous in the firelight. "You taking requests, Mister Man?" Bob gave a thumbs-up. "Ask him anything," she said to me. "You won't stump the band."

I asked for an easy one first—the Beatles' "Two of Us"—then a Joni Mitchell and a Jimmy Cliff. When Bob didn't know the lyrics he whistled, and his whistle was bolder and louder than his soulful voice. We sang Melanie's "Rollerskate Song" with bouncy irony. As we came to the la-la-la-la-la part, something caught my eye. A shadow of a figure, or an actual figure—a prowler maybe, creeping along the edges of the house, though the back gate hadn't opened or closed. At least I hadn't noticed it. The thing seemed to shimmer. Ghost? Shape-shifter? I pointed, eyes wide.

Then a full-blown person stepped into the light. "Amira!" Wendy said. "What are you doing? You scared poor Thea half to death."

"I didn't want to interrupt—" But Josie started barking, hackles up and teeth bared. I hadn't heard her bark yet. I admit I was impressed. I dragged her by the collar to the house, apologizing. Amira smiled indulgently.

She was carrying what looked like dry cleaning. The plastic bag, lit from behind by a streetlight, had created that eerie glow. Amira was tall, vivid, a Roman princess, but close up her mouth and eyes were too large for her olive face, her eyebrows too black, cheekbones too sharp. "She's a knockout—from the balcony," my father would say. And *Amira*. What kind of name was that for this moll? She should be named Dominique or Angelica. I shivered as I walked past her, as if she were a chill in the air.

I shut the back door and we shook hands, hers cool and dry, the fingernails painted a dark purple that matched her shirt. I found myself ducking my head submissively. Her voice was rich and warm, throaty. "Wendy's niece, huh?" I explained about my trip, adding that I'd be leaving in a day or two, as if I were imposing on her.

"You stay as long as you want," Wendy said. She offered Amira a piece of pie.

"No thanks. I just stopped by to bring you the dress."

Wendy had to attend a fancy dinner celebrating the college's centennial and needed semiformal attire. "Which means a black cocktail dress. Of which I own exactly none."

"And of which I own exactly seven," Amira said. "Here's the best of the bunch." She slipped the plastic from the dress, as if deftly peeling back skin.

Wendy held the dress at arm's length. "I don't know, Amira. I'm bigger than you are."

"It's got an empire waist. Very forgiving. Go try it on."

Amira and I carried dishes inside. Bob disappeared, ostensibly to put away his guitar, but the smell of pot soon drifted into the kitchen. Josie stood at attention in the living room, warming up her vocal cords for a repeat performance. I shushed her, but Amira shushed me.

"Josie," she said, in her seductive voice. "Let's get over ourselves, shall we?" She took a piece of roll from a plate and knelt down on the kitchen floor. Josie looked at her doubtfully, then at me. I waved her forward. "Come on, baby," Amira cooed. "I'm not going to hurt you. Come see me." I liked Amira then, crouched on the floor in her denim skirt, her glossy hair blue-black in the light, like Veronica in the *Archie* comics. I stood behind her, a stage mother coaching her reluctant child from the wings. Amira's purple shirt lifted as she leaned forward, exposing the small of her back. Peach fuzz, they call it. Except this fuzz wasn't peach-like. A shadow of black downy hair ran along her spine. Couldn't you wax, I thought? Use Nair?

Josie approached sideways, crab-like, and finally got close enough to snatch the bread from Amira's hand. She did it so fast, she nipped a finger. Amira fell back on her haunches, nearly landing on my feet.

"Josie!" I yelled, but she scurried down the hall with her peace offering. "Amira, I'm so sorry. Are you bleeding? Can I get you a Band-Aid?"

"She didn't break the skin," she said, examining her finger. "She's had her shots, right?"

I told her I'd just found Josie that morning. I offered Amira my hand, but she rose to her feet unassisted. "You'd better get her to the vet, Thea, if it turns out you've got a biter on your hands." She pronounced my name *Thay-ah*. I didn't bother correcting her. At that point, I assumed I'd never see her again.

Wendy emerged from the bedroom, yanking at the dress like a tomboy going to church. "Everything all right? I heard a commotion."

"Josie and I were making friends. She got a little excited, that's all."

"You do have that effect on people," Wendy said. Amira rolled her eyes. She made a twirling motion with her hand, and Wendy obliged with a coquettish spin, then stopped and tugged at the neckline. "It's a little tight across the bust."

"Quit fussing. You're going to wreck my dress. And anyway, you look fabulous. Doesn't she?"

I concurred, though black wasn't Wendy's color. She'd need bronze foundation, darker lipstick, heavy eyeliner. She modeled three pairs of shoes: brown clogs, white sandals, pink flats. She couldn't afford to buy a pair just for this occasion, and no one she knew wore a 10½. We settled on the flats.

"I've got to run," Amira said. "I have a bunch of briefs to review before tomorrow. Have a good time at the ball, Cinderella." The two women embraced, and Wendy went to her bedroom to change.

Amira put her hand on the doorknob, then turned back toward me. I crossed my arms self-consciously. "You remind me of someone." A softness in her voice surprised me. "I can't put my finger on it." She smiled, shook her head. "Do be careful out there, Thay-ah. Bad things happen to young girls traveling alone."

I nodded. "Again—I'm sorry about—"

"Don't give it another thought." She lifted her hand to display her intact finger.

As soon as the door shut, I collapsed on the couch. All I'd done for the last half hour, it seemed, was apologize. Wendy returned to the living room, Josie at her heels, and sat next to me. I told her what happened, and she laughed and scratched Josie's ears. "Did the mean lady scare you, sweet girl? Well, don't you worry. You're safe here with me."

"I *should* take her to the vet, though." I hadn't fully considered all the adult stuff I needed to face now: vaccines and how to check the oil and where to buy health insurance and what my blood type was, my tax bracket, my credit score. Did I even have a credit score? My eyes welled up. Wendy put her arm around me.

"Not to worry. I'm sure Josie doesn't have rabies. Of course she doesn't. I'll make an appointment with the vet, and we'll get everything taken care of. I've got work tomorrow, but you should go with Bob on his rounds. You'll have a great time. Jimmy is a love."

"It isn't just the rabies," I said and started crying for real. I told Wendy about my parents selling the house and how I couldn't possibly live with them in their stupid camper but I didn't know what else to do. I didn't mention Eddie. I pushed him back into a dark corner of my mind. "I'm too old to feel like an orphan."

"Never too old for that," Wendy said, patting my knee. "And anyway, what's the hurry? Stay here. The guest room is yours. Stay all summer, if you like. Or if you get tired of Bob and me bickering, we'll find you a sublet. There are plenty around, and jobs too, with the college kids gone for the summer. Thea sweetheart. We're *family*." She pressed her cheek against mine.

So there I was, stumbling upon a Plan B without even trying. It wouldn't be the first time.

PLEASE LEAVE
A MESSAGE

BOB HAD THREE OR four friends in the country who'd set up pens on their land for injured animals. His current charges included a wildcat whose leg had been caught in a trap, a red-tailed hawk shot by a hunter, a litter of orphaned baby raccoons, and an owl with a broken wing. We drove around in his truck, listening to the radio and delivering sacks of feed, bottles of sheep's milk, and dead things for the carnivores (he had a cooler filled with bags of frozen baby chicks—*chicksicles*, he called them—and some "choice roadkill"). Our last stop was Jimmy's place, about ten miles outside of Merdale. Two-lane highway, then dusty gravel county road.

"So if an owl ever takes hold of your arm with its talons, don't try to pull him off," Bob said, apropos of nothing.

I smiled. He'd hardly said a word, and now this advice. "What are you supposed to do?"

"First, if you're dealing with an owl, or any bird of prey, you should be wearing a heavy glove, like that one." He jerked his head to the bed of the pickup. A Darth Vader–like glove sat on top of a plastic milk crate full of tools and supplies. "But if for some reason, who knows why, you weren't wearing the glove, and the owl got his talons into your forearm and you tried prying him off, he'd just dig deeper. You don't want that."

"No," I agreed. We drove by a farm, where five or six horses grazed behind a white fence.

"You get a blanket or something, a towel, you know, whatever, and put it over his head. And he'll let go."

"Just like that?"

"Well, it might take a minute. But that's the proper course of action."

"Good to know," I said.

"Right?"

"Absolutely."

We listened to the radio, and he played guitar chords on the steering wheel. Jimmy's house was at the end of a long, bumpy dirt lane off the gravel road. The lane dipped and curved, following a creek lined with trees. A green hill rose up ahead, with the house and barn set against it. The house was a simple A-frame structure to the left of the lane. The barn was on the right. In front of the barn was a large vegetable garden, and in the middle of the garden stood a man wearing a straw hat and overalls. "There's James," Bob said and parked the truck in the shade.

James—Jimmy—whoever—removed the hat from his head and pulled a red bandana from a pocket to wipe off his neck and face. I remembered my Mini Mart cowboy and wondered if all the western boys carried bandanas on their person.

"Hey," he called as we climbed out of the truck.

"I've got Eli's dinner," Bob called back. Eli was the owl. All the animals had names: Scarlet the wildcat, Caleb the hawk. Bob had released a coyote named Jasper the week before.

We all walked toward each other. Jimmy's white-blond hair was matted with sweat. His skin was the fair kind that tans gradually into a golden butterscotch. He wasn't wearing a shirt under the overalls, and his arms were toned and defined, the muscles of outdoor labor, not barbells. I do love good arms on a man.

Bob introduced me. "Thea," Jimmy repeated, smiling. He seemed to taste my name in his mouth. "I'm Jimmy. Welcome to Kansas."

"Thanks. It's nice to be here."

"I like your hair."

"I like yours, too," I said.

He laughed—you could tell he was used to making disarming comments to girls, the kind of comment that would make them blush or stutter, and I had surprised him. All I can tell you is that my feeling about Jimmy was instant and irrevocable, like a flash of recognition.

Mine.

Jimmy and Bob were talking about Eli's progress and we were heading back to the truck to get owl food, and then we were walking to the pen behind the barn where the stern, yellow-eyed bird sat on a broken tree limb that Bob had placed there for him, but I was focusing on not saying something dumb, on walking without falling down, on how my face looked and my hair and my legs and my butt. I was listening to the men talk, but I was also watching Jimmy, watching him watch me, gauging his reactions. When Bob tossed some mousetrap-flattened mice into the pen, I didn't react the way I would have an hour, ten minutes, before. I didn't think, Poor little mice. I was too busy wondering if Jimmy had a girlfriend.

We sat on his front deck, and he served us sun tea—iced tea that you make by placing tea bags in big jars of water and letting it steep in the sun all day. Probably everyone knows about sun tea. I'd never heard of it before.

"How long you staying in Merdale?" he asked.

"Longer than originally planned. I was supposed to house-sit for my parents back east, but they sold the house."

He laughed. "There must be more to that story." He was sitting on an overturned wooden crate, his elbows leaning on his knees. His face was open, with even features and light blue eyes. His short swirly hair looked feather-soft. He didn't seem to have any awareness of his good looks. He was comfortable in his skin, but not cocky. This is a rare thing in a boy.

"There is, but it's not very interesting."

"You're Wendy's niece. There's no way you could possibly be uninteresting."

We flirted like that awhile. I asked him about the house, how long he'd lived there. He and Bob exchanged a look. The house was almost a year old, Bob said. "Jimmy built it himself."

"With a little help from my friends, right, Bob?"

"James is good about keeping his help happy."

I wondered if this was a reference to drugs or alcohol or free meals or all of the above. Maybe, given his easy manner, how at home he was in the world, maybe that was enough to keep his friends happy. It could keep me happy, I stupidly thought.

I asked for a tour. I wanted to get inside to see if I could find any trace of girl. Bob said he'd hang out on the porch, enjoy the view, stop and smell the roses. The joint was lit before we shut the door.

The A-frame reminded me of a huge tent, that triangular shape, steep roof on either side. Decks and windows stretched along the front and back. The entryway led to the kitchen and opened to a living room off to the left. A guest room, bathroom, and laundry room were on the right. Upstairs a loft-like balcony looked over the living room. In the bedroom the windows offered views of hills and fields and trees; the room seemed to float. I noted the antique iron headboard, the queen-sized bed with rumpled sheets, a sky-blue quilt pushed to one side. A heap of clothes was piled on a chair in the corner. I was glad Jimmy didn't apologize about the mess.

As we walked through the rooms I looked for signs of a female presence. Sure enough, a large plastic tortoiseshell barrette lay on the windowsill above the kitchen sink. A navy-blue cardigan hung on a hook by the door, and a pair of Keds was lined up next to Jimmy's work boots in the laundry room. I excused myself to use the bathroom and found a telltale box of Tampax sitting smugly in the cabinet under the sink. No visible methods of birth control, though that didn't necessarily mean anything. I surmised that this woman, whoever she was, didn't live there but visited often enough to leave behind a trail of belongings. Placeholders, marking her territory. *Stay back.* I would've done the same thing. I washed my hands and wondered at the person reflected back at me in the mirror. The haircut made my eyes look larger and my smile wider. My collarbone was too pronounced. I would have to remember to eat.

Back in the kitchen, Jimmy leaned against the island. A smooth wooden bowl held a few paper clips, a button, car keys, loose change. I asked him about the history textbooks stacked on his counter, and he told me he was an instructor at the college. He was teaching a summer class on early American utopian communities. He'd been working on a PhD in American Studies at the state university an hour away, but he'd abandoned his dissertation, "for the time being anyway." I imagined him in the classroom, strolling up and down the aisles with an open book in hand, calling on the shy girls who had crushes on him. I watched his mouth as he talked. I could picture him working in a record store. He'd be the cute guy who knew about all the obscure alternative bands. He'd remember your tastes, and every time you walked into the store he'd have a new record for you. Or a sculptor, someone who routinely put his hands into earth and clay, streaks of slip on his face. Produce from his garden sat on the tile counter. He fidgeted, picking up a pea pod or carrot now and then. His fingernails were black from yard work, his palms callused. I had to work hard to stay focused, to stop myself from imagining those good dirty hands on me, because if I continued thinking along those lines, I would lose the thread of this very basic conversation.

He asked again about my plans. "I'm supposed to deliver the car I'm driving to my friend's brother in New York," I explained. *Supposed to. Friend's brother.* I could feel the shift. I was assigning Eddie this new, safe role. *Friend's brother* was all he was to me now, and I owed him nothing except the Buick, not even an explanation. Friend's brother: someone I could flick away with one finger, a stray crumb on the table, a mild concern that didn't much concern me. I was ashamed but also thrilled. How easy, to alter the shape of things. How simple, to simply change my mind.

"The car's been leaking oil," I said. "I need to get it serviced before I leave."

"I have a friend who's a mechanic in town. He'll give you a good deal." He found a piece of scrap paper in a drawer and wrote down a name and a number. We stood close enough to each other that I could inhale his good smell, grassy and peppery. Then he turned the paper over and wrote down his number. "And call me. If you get tired of Wendy's tofu skewers."

I thanked him and took the square of paper. When our fingertips touched, there was this electric *zing*, a current that ran all the way up my arm then traveled through my chest and down my belly and hips and legs. The air around our bodies was charged, a magnetic force field, electrons and so forth bashing into each other like the air before a storm. A pheromone storm. We looked at each other, surprised, so that I knew he felt it, too. He said something involuntary, like *man oh man*, but I couldn't hear him because of the loud buzzing noise in my head from the sudden dump of hormones into my bloodstream.

"I better go now," I said, stumbling toward the door, dizzy and flushed. "Come back soon."

I couldn't look at him. If I made eye contact, I might do something I would later regret. I remembered that barrette.

~

The next day I took the car to Jimmy's mechanic. Almost everything in Merdale was within walking distance. I wandered through downtown and found my way to the college campus, which was tiny compared to the sprawling university I'd attended. The older buildings were made of native limestone, yellowish-whitish-grayish in color. The library and gym were brick. There was the usual quad with its brochure-ready expanse of green lawn and shade trees and memorial benches with names on plaques. On a bulletin board in the Student Union I scanned notices for apartment sublets and summer jobs, ads for tutoring centers and concerts, hotline numbers for the suicidal and the assaulted. All of it felt like any campus, anywhere.

Back at Wendy's I decided to call Eddie. I was taking the cowardly route; I knew he'd still be at work. Bob and Wendy weren't home yet either, so at least I'd have some privacy. The wall phone had one of those long coiled cords, and I sat at the kitchen table winding it around my wrist. *Eddie here*, his answering machine said. *Please leave a message.* Hearing his voice—for a second I had a hard time finding my own. "It's me," I finally said, "it's Thea, and I'm having problems with the car, I'm not sure how long it'll take to get it fixed, and I'm staying at my aunt's not house-sitting for my parents after all because they, um, sold the house, so anyway I'll do what I can but don't count on me because it might be a while, hope you're well, okay, bye."

Or something like that. I didn't leave a number where I could be reached. I didn't want to be reached. I wanted the whole thing done and over.

I unwound the cord, which had become tangled around my arm. Then I bravely called Jimmy.

"Took you long enough," he answered. He didn't even say hello first.

"Do you even know who this is?"

"Are you kidding? What's 'Thea' short for, anyway?"

"I can't possibly tell you."

"Athena? Althea? Theodora? Dorothea?"

"Bingo."

"I thought you couldn't tell me."

"You guessed. You *have* to tell if the person guesses. That's the rule."

"Dorothea ... ," he said. I could hear the smile in his voice. "It's the name of a much older and fatter person, don't you think?"

"As is Dottie, Dot, Dorrie. Thea's the best I could do. Though when I was little, I insisted everyone call me *Cerulean*."

"Precocious."

"I found it in my mother's oil paints. Anyway, that's not at all why I called."

"So let me guess again. The reason you're calling me is ... you're wondering how Eli's getting along?"

"Amazing. It's like ESP."

"He's doing well. He misses you, though. He was wondering when you were coming for another visit."

"No time soon, as my car's with your mechanic. Who says hi, by the way."

"I'll come get you. How about dinner? Tomorrow night?"

I smiled. "I happen to be free."

"Good. I have some friends coming, too. You'll like them."

My heart sank. I didn't want other people there. But at least they'd curb me from acting too quickly. "Animal friends or human friends?"

"Human. Nick and Julie. And Julie may even have a job for you, if you want it."

"You run a full-service operation, don't you? Car mechanics, jobs, dinner. What next?"

"Name it."

I laughed. "What time tomorrow?"

He'd pick me up early, at five o'clock, after he'd gone to the market (he called the grocery store the market). "You can help cook if you want, or just stand in the kitchen looking pretty."

"You sure are a smooth talker."

"Only when I'm in wooing mode. This is me, wooing you. Consider yourself wooed."

"Woo away. I'll see you tomorrow."

I didn't think to ask him what the job was, or to consider whether I even wanted a job, or why he was wooing me when another woman's hair accessory had taken root on his windowsill. It didn't matter. I was going to see him again.

I busied myself in the kitchen making dinner for Bob and Wendy—a curried rice salad and fresh peas—but I kept hearing Eddie's voice. *Eddie here, please leave a message.* Yes, technically, I'd taken care of the situation. But I could see what I was doing, the obvious beeline I was making for Jimmy. Eddie and Jimmy sat perched, one on each shoulder, the known and the unknown, past and present. *Eddie here. Please leave a message. Eddie here . . .*

Eddie was waiting for me. He thought I was on my way. He had this wild notion that we were actually together, the two of us, and I understood where he got that idea; yes, sure, it wasn't completely outlandish, but the truth is we'd gotten our signals crossed. And I'm no good at the uncrossing part.

I could see Emily, standing on her atoll—though she wasn't there yet, she was training in Singapore for another week—still, that's what I imagined, Emily under a palm tree, zinc oxide on her nose and hands on her hips, scolding me in fluent Yapese, then turning her back on me once and for all.

CHAPTER 3

WHAT ELSE WOULD BE THE WIND?

I FIRST STAYED WITH the Gallaghers the summer after my freshman year at Spalding, the boarding school where Emily and I met. My parents were spending the month of June at an artists' colony in Montauk, working on one of their famous collaborations (one part performance art, one part visual art, one part embarrassing). So, I could hang around Montauk. Or I could return to the Quakers. Or I could stay with my other grandparents in their one-bedroom house in Teaneck, New Jersey, television blasting fifteen hours a day and only a living room couch to sleep on.

Two weeks before the end of the term, while we sunned ourselves on the Spalding lawn and listened to a mixed tape that I'm sorry to tell you included both Peter Frampton and the Captain & Tennille, I presented the problem to Emily. She was already good at telling me what to do.

"Come home with me," she said, simply.

"Just like that? Don't you have to ask your parents?"

They loved the idea. So when the parent brigade arrived on a Saturday in June to collect their children, the Gallaghers came for Emily and me, and we drove to their estate in the New Hampshire countryside.

I'd perfected the role of houseguest over the years. I was polite but not fawning, deferential but not devoid of personality, interested in my hosts' lives but not unduly, disclosing just enough details about my own background to satisfy without piquing further interest. In the cleaned-up version of my life, my parents were loving but busy, and above all grateful to my hosts for acting *in loco parentis.*

I liked Mr. and Mrs. Gallagher, though they seemed to do a lot of play-acting. I know that sounds absurd, since I'm an expert in that department. But they often made a production out of ordinary tasks, like setting the table or walking the dog. Breakfast involved elaborate embraces and exclamatory remarks over sunburned noses or painted toenails. Mrs. Gallagher changed clothes every evening for dinner, as if we were in turn-of-the-century England, and the men would later retire to the drawing room to drink port and smoke cigars. Mr. Gallagher insisted on teaching us Latin declensions and how to play canasta. He recited Tennyson poems while washing his Porsche every Saturday. His favorite was "Lady Clara Vere de Vere." Emily insisted her parents were sincere, but I found their relentless enthusiasm exhausting.

One morning after a neighbor's cocktail party, I detected purple shadings of a hickey blooming on Mrs. Gallagher's neck—covered with Erace, for sure, but a hickey nonetheless. That same week Mr. Gallagher showed up for dinner with a slur in his speech and knocked over his water goblet. Emily and Eddie didn't pick up on what to me were the most obvious clues in the world. I played along. I knew the rules.

The first time I saw Eddie, then, was that summer. He was seventeen and went to a prestigious boys' boarding school in Massachusetts. So this family never spent any time together except during vacations, and you could tell. Not just by their formal manner, but by the constant references to a dozen things that happened when Eddie and Emily still lived at home, and everyone actually knew each other. These stories were told and retold in relay race fashion, each person taking a different leg, passing the baton to the next member of the team. ("No, no, *you* tell that part, you tell it so much better.") The details were frayed from so much handling.

The house had one of those cinematic lawns that slope gently down to a lakeshore. Emily and I spent the month swimming and sunning on the private dock. We slathered oil on each other's backs and doused our hair with lemon juice, like a couple of roaster chickens. Sometimes we walked the two miles to the village to get ice cream or drove into Concord with Mrs. Gallagher to see a movie or to shop. These were pleasant days indeed, nearly Norman Rockwellish, if you didn't pay attention to the hickeys and all.

Eddie had his own friends and his own car, so we didn't see him much. He was handsome in a nerdy AP Biology kind of way. His hair was wavy and dark brown, and he parted it far over to one side in the style of the day. He wore English Leather cologne and a braided leather belt through his cutoff shorts. A birthmark the size of a large thumbprint sat just above his left hip. He played lacrosse and tennis, took lengthy notes on his assigned summer reading (*A Separate Peace, Catch-22, The Great Gatsby*, the usual homage to masculine blah blah blah), and studied the college brochures that arrived almost daily in the mail. Sometimes he drank a few beers, but mostly he was straitlaced and smart and polite, not at all my type.

He acted as if he didn't notice me that summer, just a perfunctory "hi" at the breakfast table. We didn't have a conversation alone until I was about to leave for home.

"Emmie tells me"—he called his sister Emmie—"that you're quite the actress." We were sitting on the patio, drinking iced tea. A family of ducks had landed on the lake the day before. They paddled around in circles.

I'd always gotten the lead at Spalding. "It's in the blood I guess."

"I'll bet you look good on stage."

"What?"

"Nothing. Just, I bet you look pretty."

"As opposed to how I look off stage?"

He took his lemon slice out of his glass and squirted it at me.

"Eddie," I said, standing up. "You're embarrassing me." I smiled and went inside to finish packing. But I wasn't embarrassed. I wasn't interested in Eddie, not that summer, and not the summer after that.

Things changed during our most recent Christmas break. Emily and I were seniors in college, and Eddie was in his second year of medical school. The age difference was negligible. We hung out together, like cousins or childhood neighbors. Once or twice I caught Eddie smiling at me, his head cocked as if he'd caught me doing something adorable (unlikely). He sat next to me when we watched TV. He helped me do the dishes when it was my turn. Normally Emily would've noticed this blip on the radar, but she wasn't feeling well. Turned out she had pneumonia and stayed in bed for the last week of vacation.

Eddie and I were left to ourselves. We went to a movie. He taught me to drive a stick shift. I accompanied him to Manchester one afternoon to buy snow tires. When we were away from the house, he put his arm around me. I didn't stop him. Buddy-buddy, I thought. But I knew better.

The master suite, where, I imagined, the Gallaghers clung desperately to the opposite edges of their king-size bed, was downstairs. The kids had the upstairs. One night I went to the walk-in linen closet. The blanket I needed was on a top shelf, and it took some maneuvering to reach it. I turned around to find Eddie standing behind me. I wasn't startled. Maybe I even expected him. He took a tentative step toward me. I nodded. The kissing went on for a while. I kept my eyes open, while his were squeezed shut. He took off my T-shirt and shut the door, and we—well, the word "fornicated" applies here. Necessary, primal, uninvolved. At least, that's how I saw it.

For the rest of Christmas break we met in that closet—the safest place, farthest from Emily's room, though she was zonked on codeine and impervious to our carrying on.

"I can't believe we're doing this," Eddie whispered, the second time we were doing it. He was behind me. I was leaning on the shelves, which Mrs. Gallagher had labeled with her label maker. QUEEN FITTED, QUEEN TOP, QUEEN PILLOWCASE. We paused for the finish then sat on the floor.

"I can't believe it either." Jean Naté and fabric softener hung in the air. Mrs. Gallagher, I was sure, added Downy to every load and breathed in the towels like the lady on the commercial, as if they were fresh air itself. "Emily would kill me."

"She wouldn't. She loves us both. Though"—he hastened to add—"we should probably keep this to ourselves." No one had ever made me feel cheap before, but Eddie was getting close.

He veered into another subject. He was dreading the new semester, he said. He'd heard horror stories about the pharmacokinetics instructor. He often felt overwhelmed, he couldn't deal with the pressure. He'd nearly flunked one of his finals. Maybe medical school wasn't such a great idea.

"You're just burned out," I assured him. "It's normal to feel this way. Hang in there. You'll be okay." The truth was that medical school wasn't optional. Eddie's father was a doctor, and his grandfather, and probably a grandfather or two before that.

He sighed. "You're a nice girl, Thea."

"No I'm not."

"You're nicer than you think."

"Well, that's certainly possible."

I put my Pretenders T-shirt back on. If you married Eddie, I mused, you would not wear a Pretenders T-shirt to bed. You'd wear white lacy nightgowns that his mother gave you for your birthday, and he'd watch shyly as you changed, and that look (eyes cast downward, then up again, almost eyelash-batting) would be the signal for sex. I shook myself free of these thoughts. Eddie remained slumped on the floor. I wondered if he was taking drugs. Maybe he was the type to do drugs and get morose instead of happy. Some people were like that, I knew. I opened the door a crack, as if we were playing a game of spies. Every night the floorboards of the old house threatened to give up our secret, like a tattletaling little brother. "The coast is clear," I said in a stage whisper. I tiptoed back to the guest room, where I had spent so much time that the Gallaghers kept framed photos of me and Emily and Eddie on the dresser, as if I were part of that family and not the slutty interloper meeting their son for trysts in the tidy and fresh-smelling closet every night.

Emily and I returned to California, and Eddie started calling me. He must've known her schedule—he only called when she was out. Sometimes he was anxious, and I learned to console him. I liked being the one to coax the other person away from the cliff's edge. It was a nice change of scenery. Also, my understanding of the world is, at best, impressionistic. I get the general gist. But Eddie knew how things work. He retained actual information, facts, trivia. I could ask him to explain about the moon and the tides, or the difference between stocks and bonds, or how to plot stars on a graph to make a Hertzsprung-Russell diagram (who knew Astronomy was going to require math?). I came up with questions and then lay back and listened to his answers. He had the voice of a late-night DJ playing jazz for the insomniacs.

The last time he called—the night before I left California—he'd been taking Dexedrine for two days straight, cramming for exams. Emily didn't hear the phone ring; she was cleaning out the fridge and the radio was on. Still, I had to be careful.

"This isn't a good time," I whispered.

"I wanted to catch you before you left. You're heading out tomorrow?"

"First thing."

"Okay. I'll get right to the point. I know you're supposed to house-sit for your parents this summer, but I was thinking—maybe you and I should try living together."

I hadn't told him about my housing crisis. I'd only just found out myself. Plus, I was afraid he'd offer me the very thing he was now offering me. I tried to interject.

"Wait," he said. "Hear me out."

And maybe it was the stress or the speed or the sleep deprivation, but he was off and running. This was a whole other Eddie. He had a lot of ideas, and they all came tumbling out at once. I could apply for graduate school in the fall. He'd picked up course catalogs and applications from NYU and Columbia. I wanted to go to graduate school, right? (It's possible I said something along those lines at some point.) Also he'd been reading the Help Wanted ads. There were jobs "right here in White Plains," or I could commute into the city. On the weekends, we could spend time at my folks' house if I wanted to, or head to New Hampshire or Block Island—he had friends who had friends who had a house on the beach. We could go to Shakespeare in the Park and Tanglewood and Coney Island. He'd made a calendar of events. The possibilities were endless!

I kept my eyes on the swinging kitchen door. It's hard to object in a whisper. I couldn't say his name or anything else loudly enough to stop him. I looked around helplessly. He started in on the subject of us. *Us.* I wondered if I should hang up. I'd never seen any point in telling Eddie about my casual and intermittent affair with Danny, but now it seemed like one of those sins of omission people talk about. Danny and I would be spending that night together. Our *Schwanengesang*, Danny called it. Swan song.

The 5th Dimension played on the kitchen radio, and Emily began singing along. I grabbed the opportunity. "*Eddie,*" I said in my loudest stage whisper. But he just kept going. "You and I get along so great," he said, "we can talk about anything, and the sex—wow, the sex is just the best ever, and we have this shared history, it all just makes so much sense. Emily will be thrilled, or at least she'll come around. We can wait to tell her. We can change our story just a little. We can say that one thing led to another, which would be true, and that we got together over the summer, which would also be true in a way, and regardless she'll have the whole year in Micronesia to get used to the idea.

"I'm ready to take the next step," he said. "Thea, I love you. I'm in love with you. I want to marry you."

"*What?*" I said. Too loud.

"What?" Emily called. She turned down the radio. I froze. "Everything okay out there?"

"Yes," I said. "Everything's fine."

But it wasn't fine. Something had happened or continued to happen on the other end of the line. "I'm just so happy you're coming home," Eddie said. He sounded like he was weeping. "I know you can't talk right now. It's okay. You don't need to say a word. I understand. And I promise I'll propose properly when you get here. A proper proposal promised!" He giggled. This was all so not-Eddie.

I've never done well with declarations of love. Emily used to say it's because I like the chase. "As soon as you catch the guy, you don't know what to do with him. He says he loves you, you start looking for the door." Maybe so. But I didn't chase Eddie. I thought Eddie was safe. I thought we had an understanding. Now he'd put us into this whole other category, and we could never go back. I'd lost him as a friend, and if Emily found out, I'd probably lose her, too. At the same time, I knew he was not in his right mind. Once he came to his senses he'd be horrified.

Emily pushed open the swinging door.

"Sorry," I said into the receiver. "You have the wrong number."

"I just—I can't wait to see you, Thea," Eddie said. And there was something in his voice. My breath caught, in spite of myself.

"No problem," I said and hung up.

"What'll it be for dinner?" Emily held up a pizza coupon in one hand and a bag of soba noodles in the other. She would want to use up everything in the pantry before moving out. I pointed at the noodles. She rewarded me with a smile and turned back to the kitchen.

I unplugged the phone. Service would be disconnected at midnight anyway. I smoothed the Indian bedspread that covered the futon couch. The red and gold throw pillows from the head shop downtown had shiny sequins sewn on them. I lifted a pillow and tried to see my face in one of the tiny diamond-shaped mirrors. The pillow was Danny's. He was a trust fund kid. Everything was his. The chef's knife that Emily was using at that moment to chop garlic. The cutting board. The silverware, plates, appliances, futon, scatter rugs, the apartment itself, which was on the second floor of his house, prime real estate two blocks from the ocean. Danny was one of those lucky people.

The next morning Emily and I loaded the last of my stuff into her car. Danny sat on the front steps, shirtless as usual, reading Wittgenstein's *On Certainty* and stroking his beard. When it was time for me to go, Emily and I cried and carried on, but Danny just lifted his mug of chai to me, winked, and went inside. About what I expected.

Anyway. I didn't call Eddie right back. I could've found a pay phone on my way out of town and called him collect. But the more I thought about the conversation, the more confused I felt. On the one hand, it was outrageous. He wanted us to get *married*? We weren't even dating, or whatever! I'd just graduated from college! He had always been rational and disciplined, like his sister, but now he had put me in this terrible position. It was embarrassing. And irritating, too.

On the other hand. *I just can't wait to see you, Thea.* Such longing. Had anyone ever expressed such longing for me before?

I decided I'd call him from the road. Or no, I'd wait until I got there. Some conversations should only take place in person. I promised myself I would not spend the night with him, no matter how easy or harmless it would seem at the time, no matter how much we drank. Sleep with him now, I warned myself, and in five years you'll end up divorced and living on alimony. And that does *not* qualify as a backup plan. It does not.

~

I served the curry dinner, and afterward Wendy and Bob invited me to a jam session at a friend's house, but I wasn't in the mood. I took Josie for a walk around Merdale Town Park. The park was a neat square, each side a quarter mile long and lined with enormous oaks and elms. It sat between downtown and Campus Corner, where the college hangouts were located. The park was a happy, busy place. Tennis and basketball courts, playground, swimming pool, butterfly garden, baseball field. The field was lit up, Little Leaguers at bat. Voices called out *atta kid, atta kid* and *batterbatterbatterbatterbatter*. An ice-cream truck sold frozen treats. Parents pushed kids in strollers, greeted me, asked to pet the dog. The air was balmy soft. I still felt like shit.

Back at Wendy's I found a piece of paper and sat at the table in my room. I made two columns. Pros. Cons. Emily usually did this part. She called it The Lesser of Two Evils game. She'd get out her clipboard and pen and paper, peering at me over her glasses. Nothing gave her greater pleasure than a good list. Prom date: Joey or Michael? College: California or Vermont? Major: Psychology or English? She loved the rational approach, but she also loved the random, the mystical. She threw the I Ching, she laid out tarot cards, she propped her Ouija board on her lap. She'd narrow her gaze at my future, tapping with her index finger, making her funny pursed-lips sound. "There you have it," she'd tap, even when "there" and "it" still seemed unclear to me. For Emily, everything had a right or wrong answer, and she knew which was which. But I couldn't stay inside the lines. I don't mean that in a creative, do-whatever-you-want-in-your-coloring-book way.

"All right, Em, here goes," I whispered, as if conjuring one of her Ouija spirits. Nothing had happened with Jimmy yet, I reasoned. If I felt conflicted about Eddie, I should take a closer look. I owed it to him. I congratulated myself on my maturity.

I wrote EDDIE GALLAGHER at the top of the page. I started with the Pros. "He's in love with me," I said. Josie wagged her tail. "And that's always or almost always or at least sometimes a good thing." Right away I could see all sides of that story. "Anyway. We'll put that on the Plus side for now. Okay. He's ..." I thought for a minute and started writing. He's dependable. Yes—rock solid. He's loyal. He's kind. He has a roof over his head, so I'd have one over mine, which would be dandy. We have a history together, as he'd pointed out. Isn't that supposed to be an important thing? *And* ... (I saved best for last) he's already popped the question. I wrote that down—*engaged*—and didn't bother with quotation marks. I knew what I meant. I counted up what I had so far. Seven things.

I moved to the Cons. I tapped the pen against my teeth. This game was easier when you were deciding which elective course to take in your finally declared double major (Comparative Lit and Theater, with a minor in French, because why not?), or which crappy summer job. It felt mean, to halve a person.

I sighed. At the bottom of the page, I sketched Eddie's face. I drew him smiling, his eyes smiling, too. At the end of the day, you would see this face at your door and you wouldn't be sorry. You wouldn't get too tired of it. The nose—largish, but not comical. Earnest brown eyes. The slightest suggestion of a cleft chin, which helped to distract from his high forehead. I added laugh lines, parentheses around the mouth. I erased some of the hair. Here's how he would look, old.

"White Plains, New York?" I wrote under Cons. Was White Plains a Pro or a Con? I'd never been there.

"Med school/doctor?" The other column didn't have any of these annoying question marks.

Under both columns, right above the drawing of Eddie's face, I wrote in big spread-out letters: E ... M ... I ... L ... Y.

Nothing on that list made much sense to me. Eddie. Eddie, Eddie, Eddie. EddieEddieEddieEddie. Say it over and over and it doesn't mean anything. Look at yourself too long in the mirror and you don't look like anybody. I said his name until it sounded like yedi, yedi, yedi. I knew there wasn't any point in trying to approach the problem rationally.

"Are *feelings* and *emotions* always the wind in your sails?" Emily once asked me. What else would be the wind?

I folded the Pros and Cons list and stuck it in the zippered pocket of my suitcase with the ponytail. Maybe they'd rub together and do some magic. Maybe that explains everything that happened next.

FOLIE À DEUX

"JIMMY'S OLD HOUSE BURNED down a couple of years ago." Wendy and I were sitting on the lime-green porch swing, waiting for Jimmy to pick me up for dinner. The cats were lolling on the porch steps as usual. A couple of neighborhood kids were drawing on the sidewalk with thick colored chalk.

"Burned down?"

"I didn't know him then. I met him through Bob, and Bob and I have only been together, what, a year now."

"What was the cause of the fire?"

"I don't know if they ever determined, for sure. Maybe something electrical? But Jimmy hates talking about it. Seriously, don't bring it up. He lost everything he owned in that fire—including the only copies of his dissertation."

"That's why he never got his PhD."

"Right. All that work up in smoke."

The children were outlining each other in what looked alarmingly like those police outlines of dead bodies. Then they started filling in: facial features, clothing, hair. The boy added bulbous boobs to the girl's outline. She yelled at him to quit it. People here said "quit it" instead of "stop it." Also grocery *sacks* instead of *bags*, license *tags* instead of *plates*, *anymore* instead of *nowadays*. As in, anymore, little boys have no shame.

Wendy walked over and adjudicated. The boy apologized, sort of, and walked home. The girl continued drawing. She made a dog on a leash that looked like a giant rabbit. Wendy spoke to her in a high-pitched, loud voice, as if the girl had mental or hearing difficulties. Wendy's intense interest in children made me squeamish. This desire to breed! I couldn't imagine. Maybe when I turned thirty, I'd transform magically into a real adult and decide to put those reproductive organs to some reproductive use.

Wendy settled her considerable self on the swing and gave it a kick to get going. "Jimmy's first house belonged to his grandparents. They left it to him. He used to spend summers out there as a kid. The fire was devastating. But at least he had insurance." *IN-surance*, instead of *inSURance*. "He built the A-frame on the foundation of the old house. Bob helped some, but mostly Nick. Nick's a carpenter."

"He and Julie are going to be at dinner tonight."

"You'll meet everyone. The whole gang."

"Why are you so sure?"

"Because," she said. "It's a package deal." She smiled. A cat jumped on her lap. A soft breeze rose up. And before I could ask her what she meant, Jimmy pulled up to the curb, got out of his truck, and opened the door for me.

~

We ate dinner at Jimmy's long wooden table, and afterward Julie and I sat on the deck while Jimmy and Nick played horseshoes. Julie's brown hair was bobbed and clipped back from her dimply face with two pink plastic bow clips. One front tooth overlapped the other. She was stocky and strong and short. She rode her bike to work every day, swam a mile at the campus pool at lunch, and in winter coached a roller derby team in Topeka. I already loved her.

"Nick's been married a lot," Julie confided. She held an unlit Marlboro Light, every now and then running it under her nostrils as if preparing to smoke a fine Havana cigar.

"What's a lot?" I asked.

"I don't want to shock you."

"My parents divorced and remarried each other. Twice." This was true, and one reason I'd chosen to abscond to Spalding at age fourteen. I'd grown tired of the drama.

Julie wanted details. I described my parents as profligate artists, which is how they liked to see themselves. "The truth is, under that flighty exterior is a rock-hard core. They have a nose for good investments. But they never really grasped what parenting was about. I mean, they weren't bad parents. They love me, they've always wanted the best for me. They were just distracted. They were so caught up in their own colorful story, sometimes they forgot I was there." I smiled as if to say, "No harm done." I didn't want Julie to think I'd been neglected. It wasn't like that. I'd just been perennially left to my own devices. "Anyway, back to Nick."

Julie nodded. "He's had three wives. But the first one didn't count—they were only married for a week. He and I were friends through two of the marriages. When the last one fell apart, it's like he finally looked up and noticed me standing there, waiting for him, girlfriend material." Julie held out her arms in a ta-da! gesture. I laughed.

She lifted the unlit cigarette. "I only allow myself one a day," she said. "Sometimes I don't even light it. I just hold it. Tonight, though . . ." She took a Bic lighter from her shorts pocket with a flourish, lit the cigarette, and inhaled deliciously. When she exhaled, she made a purring mmmmm sound. We talked some more, and when she finished her cigarette, she called out to Nick. "You almost ready, Big Time?" He waved at her.

The horseshoe pit was out by the garden. Fireflies had begun to dot the dark green fields, like scattered white Christmas lights. The two handsome players were silhouetted against the barn. What a lovely sight, that pair of men out there, tossing horseshoes and laughing. Even as I was waiting for Nick and Julie to leave, I was also enjoying the scene. I felt patient and at ease and excited at the same time. I hadn't felt this good since leaving California. Things were falling into place. Julie owned a used bookstore and needed some temporary help; her college student employee had changed plans and left town for the summer. We talked about the job at dinner. She was flexible. I could assist her for a week while she found a replacement, or I could be the replacement. I laughed at the idea of staying for the whole summer, but Nick shrugged and said, "Everybody has to be somewhere." Nick, with his silvery sly good looks and his troubles in love. And with digits: he was a carpenter and had lost two fingers above the knuckle joint on his left hand, a fact I hadn't noticed until he passed me a bowl of sliced peaches and plums.

"Circular saw," he said. "Never saw it coming." He gave me his twinkly, mustachey Sam Elliott smile. There was something tender and flawed about Nick. I understood Julie's attraction. She was a sucker for damaged men. Plenty of them out there, but she wanted this one.

"It's all Jimmy's fault," Julie teased. "Nick lost his fingers while he was building this house."

"Yeah, they're around here somewhere," Nick said.

Jimmy was sitting close to me, one arm on the back of my chair. My thin cotton shirt was cut low in the back, and I could feel his skin against mine. "Let's not drag up all that ancient history," Jimmy said. "I don't want to scare Thea away."

"I'm not easily scared." But there was something in his voice, and I wondered what everyone else knew that I didn't. One of my English professors once said that there are only two stories in the world. Someone goes on a journey, or a stranger comes to town. But that's just the same plot from different viewpoints. I was the traveler, and the stranger. *One of these things is not like the other, one of these things just doesn't belong* . . . Oh, Julie and Nick and Jimmy were kind to me, they didn't exclude me or anything, but now and then they inadvertently lapsed into code, the shorthand that had developed over the years. One gesture or phrase or word signaled some shared moment, or referred to other, absent members of their tribe. I wished I could skip all the parts about getting to know people, their old stories and customs, and just be there, among them, like them, of them. For a moment I thought, What are you doing here? The car will be ready tomorrow. Just *go.*

Nick rose stiffly from the table, joints creaking and popping, old injuries from his high school football days. "You guys cooked, Jules and I will clean up," he said. When he and Julie were both at the sink, Jimmy leaned in to me and whispered, "You okay?" He'd noticed the shift. I felt reassured. "Yes," I said. "I'm good." He kissed my hair just above the ear, and the ear tingled and zinged.

Oh boy, I thought. No matter what. Here we go.

We helped with the washing up in spite of Julie's protests, and then Nick suggested a round of horseshoes so that Julie could have her cigarette and enjoy the sunset.

And then they left. Jimmy and I stood on the deck waving, as if we were already a couple. I wondered what he had told Nick and Julie about me. There's this girl I met? Wendy's niece is going to hang out with us? Or were his friends so accustomed to a new face at his table that their nonchalance was authentic, not put on for my benefit?

We watched the taillights on Julie's car bounce up and down as she navigated the gravel lane, kicking up dust, and we stood there until we couldn't hear the engine. Then Jimmy turned to me and touched my face lightly with his fingertips, as if checking to see if I was still there. When he touched me like that, so tentatively, I heard myself whimper. I cleared my throat to camouflage the sound.

"So are you—seeing anyone?" I whispered.

"No."

I didn't press him about the girl paraphernalia. And he didn't ask me about my situation. I don't think, at that moment, he cared. Or maybe he figured, what the hell, it's her decision. I wouldn't have known what to say, anyway. Come to think of it, I'm engaged? We went inside and climbed the stairs to his bedroom, the air rushing and crackling around us, charged as when our fingers brushed against each other that first time. The room was tidier than when I saw it two days before. I'll bet he changed the sheets for me, I thought. He's put away the clothes that were draped on the chair. He's swept the floor. The light was on a dimmer switch, and he already had it on low, ready for the moment when I would enter the room. I felt the apprehension in his preparations. Picturing him with a dust rag in his hand, or pulling up the bedspread, endeared him to me further. Then we were kissing, finally we were kissing, and then we were on his bed. The good smell of him—spring fields and something spicy like gingersnaps—I breathed him in. The body, the body knows what it wants, and you can't convince it of anything, you can't say, "You don't even know this person, you better not, what if . . ." But you don't care about the what ifs. The what ifs have left the premises. The premises themselves have left the premises. We were practically panting, his hands on my face, in my short hair, his mouth on my mouth, on my neck, on my eyelids, on my mouth. We kissed for a long time with our clothes on, then there was a hilarious bit where we couldn't get our clothes off fast enough.

And finally, the relief of finding each other, skin on skin. Legs wrapped around. Astonished pauses in between. Me clinging to those iron head-board bars with both hands. And then the sweet fall.

Afterward, lying there, I slowly became aware again, self occupying body, conscious of limbs, face, breath, sheets, pillow, walls. Above me was a skylight I hadn't noticed before. I waited for Jimmy to speak. I was afraid he would say something stupid. After our first linen closet encounter Eddie said, "That was super!" Like some comic book character from the 1950s. *Kablowie!* I expected Jimmy to make some witticism, the kind of distancing comment that would allow us to rise from bed and go pee or get dressed and act as if nothing significant had just happened. Like, "Isn't this the part where we have a cigarette?" or "That was certainly the highlight of my day," or some comment about *California girls*, proving how little we knew each other. Maybe for him, I was just another one-night stand. He had readied this room for me and readied himself, and now he could check me off his list. I would go back to Wendy's, and get in Emily's car, and drive to New York, and I would never see Jimmy Ward again. It would serve me right.

But mostly I was waiting because that's how I was back then. I had to know what he was feeling before I could know what I was supposed to feel.

No forest, no trees.

He lifted my hand to his lips, kissed it, eyes closed.

"Thea." He started to say something else, stopped, started again. I curled up against him. Then, almost inaudibly, he spoke. "Stay with me awhile."

～

The next day I ignored Wendy's skeptical looks and my own feeble mis-givings, like shutting the door on a prim old aunt muttering admon-ishments in the next room. I picked up the car from the mechanic and

unloaded my boxes of stuff and stored them in Wendy's garage. I took my
suitcase and my dog and drove out to Jimmy's.

Anyone would tell you that you shouldn't, ever, move in with someone you just met. I would tell you this. It's a terrible idea. Jimmy and I
were aware. "This is nuts," we agreed. We said things like "summer fling"
and "temporary insanity." *Folie à deux*. But we also didn't think of it as
me moving in. *Stay awhile* meant hang out for a week or two and see
what happens. Jimmy was throwing a summer solstice party, so I'd stick
around for that, anyway. Eddie didn't need the car. He was just storing it
in his garage until Emily's return. I'd call him at some point and check in.
I remembered his summer plans for us—Tanglewood, Coney Island—
and felt a tug or a twinge or a pang. But I swiftly suppressed my doubts.

At the extreme outside, I told myself, I'd head east by Labor Day.
That was three months away! I doubted I'd stay in Kansas a month, let
alone three.

Jimmy and I granted each other the right to renege at any time, no
explanations or apologies necessary. And if neither of us chose to back
out? We would revisit, and rewrite, the rules later. As if emotions had
nothing to do with it. As if we didn't know that explanations and apologies are always necessary.

So I sent Eddie a postcard. *Out of money. Getting a job here for a bit.
Sorry for any inconvenience. More soon.* Like a good old-fashioned tele-
gram. I didn't specify what I meant by "here." Or "sorry," or "soon." Julie
had me on the schedule at the bookstore, so at least the part about the
job was true. Once I sent that postcard I put Eddie in a box somewhere,
sealed it up, and shoved it onto a back shelf. I counted on him to stay put.

~

Julie's bookstore was located in Campus Corner, a four-square-block area
across from the college where the usual student hangouts stood shoulder
to shoulder: bars, coffee shop, a Chinese restaurant and a pizza joint, a
clothing boutique, a futon store, and a bakery where you could line up in
the alley at two in the morning after last call and a guy in a white apron
and hat would stand in the back door and sell you fresh glazed donuts

that were such a seductive blend of sugar and fat and warm melty softness that you were sure you'd never be that happy eating anything ever
again, and you'd be right. I felt like I was still in college. I kept having that
nightmare where you have to take a final exam to graduate. You haven't
studied. You've never even attended class, and in fact you have no idea
what the class is. You're looking around frantically for some clue about
the general subject area, math or history or what, while all the other students calmly take out their blue examination books and #2 pencils. You,
of course, have brought neither.

During my first couple of weeks on the job, I worked the counter and
answered the phone so Julie could catch up with the backlog, boxes and
boxes of books she needed to sort through and price. I met the regular
customers: two avid sci-fi fans, a Tony Hillerman fanatic, an atlas col-
lector, and a half-dozen women who traded in romance novels on an
almost daily basis. Julie kept a stack of books under the counter for these
loyal customers. They'd paw through the titles, pouncing when they saw
something they wanted.

Sometimes we sat on the floor going through New Arrivals, and she
showed me which books were keepers and why. I doubted I could ever
take on this task—she had the store's entire inventory in her head. "*Pride
and Prejudice* goes in the 'no' pile," she'd say. A Jane Austen class spring
semester had glutted the market. "On the Erica Jongs we'll say yes to
Fear of Flying, no to the poetry. *Malcolm X*—the pages are yellow, but
they teach it at the high school every year, so it'll sell. This copy has come
through the store a few times. I remember this name." She showed me
where the original owner had written her name in purple pen. Roald
Dahl was especially popular, but any children's book in good condition
was a keeper. "Look for *wholesome* titles for the homeschooling moms,"
she said. Every Thursday morning they descended with their broods and
held their own private story time in the children's corner. "I can sell five
or six books if I have the right ones. Series are especially good. *Amelia
Bedelia*, *Little Bear*. Like that."

She glanced at the prices on the back covers, made a quick calcu-
lation, and penciled in her price on the top of the first page. "Touch
a book once. If you pick it up and put it down, you'll never make a

decision. Decide yes or no, figure out the price, hand over the cash. Done and done."

The best part about working for Julie was her tacit approval of Jimmy and me. "Whatever makes you happy, is my feeling," she said, pausing to punch in numbers on a calculator. "I mean, who am I to judge? I've managed somehow to hover around the same guy for fifteen years—off and on—even while *he* kept marrying other people."

The sun shone through the big plate glass windows. I was proud of my Summer Reading display, complete with striped inflatable ball, umbrella, books scattered on a beach towel. I'd painted a blue-sky backdrop. *Dip into a Good Book!* My lettering was perfect.

"Do you want to marry him?"

"And be wife number 4?" She smiled. "What are the odds that'd work?" She carried a stack of books to the New Arrivals shelf and started on another box. "I'm thirty-six years old. I thought I'd have a family by now. I figured I'd live in a big city, Chicago or someplace, and I'd be, you know, a professional something, public relations or, or what? A diplomat. A travel agent. A magazine editor. I certainly did not see Merdale, Kansas, as part of my future. I didn't see running a bookstore." She waved her arms at the stacks of books, then looked out the window for a moment. She sighed. "Nick doesn't like staying with the women he marries. He likes staying with me because I won't marry him. Sick, but true."

"Maybe he'll change."

"Nope. He won't. Doesn't want to. But if he decides to go off and marry someone else, or date someone else, or *whatever* with someone else, he's on his own. I don't have time to go through all that again."

I could feel Julie's resignation. Here was a man she couldn't help but love, even if he was the wrong man. "The heart wants what it wants—or else it does not care." Emily Dickinson wrote that in a letter. I made a mental note to check the poetry section for her *Collected Poems*.

"You're young," I said. "You never know what's going to happen."

"Not that young. Not like you." She sat back in her chair, put the book she held on her lap. "It's nice here, isn't it? I love this time of day. Whenever I feel this way and look at the clock, it's always, always, 2:37, or 2:39. The afternoon changes gears. And the store is quiet. There's this lull." She smiled at me again, that front tooth overlapping the other front tooth. Her pink hair clips held back the hair from her open face.

The phone rang, and I rose to answer it. Julie leaned over her book, and as I walked behind her—without really looking, without meaning to look—I saw down her shirt. No bra. No breasts. Just a long jagged scar across the puckered skin of her chest.

CHAPTER 5

THE RELUCTANT KING

FRIDAY, THE DAY BEFORE the solstice party, I woke up to voices—the open loft of the bedroom looked on to the living room, and sound traveled. I put on a shirt and shorts and went downstairs.

A boy sat across from Jimmy at the table. When I walked in the room, he ducked his head and coughed, as if to warn his host about the girl in his house. Then he saw Josie, trotting behind me, and he pushed back his chair. "Does he bite?"

"Josie?" I laughed. "She's harmless." I put her outside for her morning constitutional. She had a whole secret life out there.

"Thea, this is George Leonard," Jimmy said. "George, this is Thea Knox. Thea is Wendy's niece."

"Sorry. I didn't know Jimmy had company."

"No need to apologize. It's nice to meet you." I sat down across from him, wanting to say, I'm not *company*—I live here. Didn't I? I *felt* at home, thanks to the happy routine Jimmy and I had already established. Every morning we stayed in bed late, then made breakfast, took Josie for a walk, and checked the garden for green beans and peas. At noon I drove into town, humming and happy, as if this were truly my life, my intended and intentional life. Jimmy taught his class at two o'clock. While Julie went for her lunchtime swim, I held down the fort. I shelved books, answered the phone, dusted, cleaned the bathroom, chatted with customers. After work Jimmy and I met for a beer, and the evening unfolded.

Even country life was becoming familiar. I'd never lived in the country. The Hudson Valley, which was only "the country" to the city folks my parents entertained on weekends, didn't count. This was rural. (*Rool.*)

Gravel roads and well water, no cable TV or gas lines for the stove or furnace. No houses nearby, at least none that you could see from his deck—the nearest neighbors were a couple of miles to the north. Just plowed fields and sky, red-tailed hawks and turkey vultures swooping high in the air, the yip of coyotes at night, deer at the edge of the creek every morning, an occasional loose cow from a neighboring ranch wandering onto Jimmy's property, the owl hooting from his pen. I learned from Jimmy's daily efforts the upkeep involved, how fences needed to be mended, gardens weeded, rock walls repaired, screens patched, cracks caulked, mildew removed, wood split for winter.

George was twelve but looked older, maybe fifteen. He was almost as tall as Jimmy, with a big blond tangled mop of hair. He shook his head as if expecting things to fall out of the curls. He had a tough time with eye contact. He did this facial thing that was maybe a nervous tic.

Jimmy brought me a cup of coffee in my favorite gray-blue mug. I already had a favorite mug. "Erika—George's mom—is an old friend," he explained. "Sometimes when she has errands to run, George hangs out with me for the day."

"It's not errands," George said. "She's at the lake, waterskiing. I don't like the water." He did the thing with his face again, putting his hand up to shield my view. "Hey, can *I* have some coffee?"

"Dude, I got in trouble last time."

"She doesn't care as long as it's before lunch."

Jimmy brought him a cup without needing to ask him how he liked it (a lot of milk and even more sugar). "George is in a band," Jimmy said to me. "The Reluctant Kings."

"Great name."

"Do you know the trilogy?" George asked. I did not. He began describing the intricate plot of a fantasy novel. He was prepared to give me a detailed synopsis.

"And there's *King* George, too," Jimmy interrupted. "They called King George VI the reluctant king."

"He stuttered," George added. "At least I don't do *that*."

"The Reluctant Kings are going to take the world by storm. They're barely out of grade school, and they're already way better than most Merdale bands."

"We've never actually performed anywhere."

"You've played out here."

"For you, and mom, and Wendy and Bob." Bob, I learned later, was his guitar teacher.

"You're twelve years old. Give it time."

George went out to the deck where he'd left his guitar and sat in the rocking chair noodling away. He did sound good.

"The Kings do a wicked cover of 'Gimme Shelter,'" Jimmy said. "They were supposed to play at a school dance last year, but George has bad stage fright. They had to bail." I wasn't surprised. George seemed pretty fragile.

Jimmy topped off my coffee, then bent down to kiss my cheek, and that was the first time he just, you know, gave me a peck and moved on. I remember it because it felt nice—just this little kiss on the cheek, a kiss of appreciation or acknowledgment, a kiss in passing, a kiss in parentheses, a kiss just because I was sitting there at his table, drinking the coffee he had made me. Very boyfriend-like. Very, we've been together for a long time-ish. He stood at the counter, his strong lovely back to me, his white-blond hair sticking up as it did sometimes, surveying the day outside the windows and listening to the guitar melodies as they floated through the screen door.

He didn't teach on Fridays, and Julie had given me the afternoon off to help Jimmy with the party. I'd looked forward to having the day at home, but now that George was here, we shifted into a different mode. Jimmy didn't mind—that's just how he was, amenable to whatever came up. He never looked back or worried that he'd wasted time. Whatever was happening was simply what was happening, and he didn't think about the things he could be doing, or should be doing, instead. "Go along to get along," he'd say. "Take the path of least resistance." But what if the path of most resistance was the right path?

Of course, I was the same way, drifting along with the current. I had put everything on hold—whatever *everything* was—and docked at Jimmy's for no other reason than our instant chemistry and my lack of options. I wasn't exactly taking charge of my life, finding a purpose, moving forward. Sometimes I looked up from sponging off the kitchen counter, or making the bed, or shelving books at the store, and felt momentarily bewildered. I'd stand for a moment, scanning the room, wondering how I'd gotten there. I had walked into someone else's life. This was not my kitchen counter, not my bed, not my house, not my car, not my job, not my town. My sense of being in the world wavered. I recalled the Bonneville Salt Flats in Utah and how they rippled in the heat, becoming lakes and sea. My life as highway mirage.

~

Jimmy spent the day working on a surprise. He mowed a big circle in the field behind the barn, and now he and George were scooping sand into small bags—dozens of them, hundreds maybe—and arranging them in some kind of pattern. I made batter for brownies, glancing out the window every now and then. From a distance the man and the boy looked about the same age. Out of nowhere they'd start wrestling, as if a bell had rung. I just love boys. Girls are so earnest, what with their empire waist dresses and plans to save the world and waiting around for boys to love them. But boys are gleefully stupid. They ride on top of cars. They build catapults and launch water balloons. They make giant snow-sculpture penises. They skateboard and bike and ski in places they shouldn't. They fill lunch bags with sand.

I talked to Emily in my head, imagining her observations about this new cast of characters. "Well," she'd say, "there's George, who's just a kid, and yet so serious. Nick—a grown man, but so childish. And Jimmy? Why, Dorothea, he's just right."

I smiled and poured the brownie batter into pans and stuck them in the oven, then picked up yesterday's newspaper and studied the classified ads. I needed a second part-time job for the mornings, preferably something short-term. Julie could only pay minimum wage, and the car repairs had eaten a large chunk of my savings (asking Eddie for reimbursement was out of the question, and I knew better than to accept the help Jimmy offered). Even though I wasn't paying rent, I needed to start a just-in-case fund. Just in case the unforeseen occurred, which it most certainly would. I'd always put aside an emergency stash, and I always ended up needing it, the kindness of strangers notwithstanding.

I made some phone calls and arranged a few job interviews for Monday. I knew I would get offers. I had a sixth sense for detecting exactly what the interviewer wanted and molding myself to that image. I often took jobs I didn't want, only to quit them a few weeks later. I hoped to be more selective this time. "Employment history" was one of those things I should start paying attention to. I did all this—circled ads, made phone calls—while ignoring what it meant. A few more weeks, I told myself. Time to regroup. That's all. But I knew the danger I was in with Jimmy. I took the brownies out of the oven and brought the men glasses of sun tea.

That night Jimmy and George and I drove into Merdale for barbecue, then went to the city park to listen to a bluegrass band. George stood in front of the stage, fingers twitching by his side as he studied the lead guitarist's every move. Little kids danced and ran around catching fireflies. Old people sat on lawn chairs, nodding their heads to the music. Couples held hands, and teenagers sneaked under the bleachers to drink beers and make out. Josie sat on our blanket, well behaved but trembling with the possibilities. The blanket was our little raft. We drifted along on fiddle tunes and Friday night and summer air. When the last encore was over, Jimmy leaned in and kissed my neck. "Now I'm going to take you home and do things to you," he whispered. I laughed. "I can't wait," I said. We drove George home. Jimmy introduced me to Erika, and she invited us in for a beer. When we declined, she smiled knowingly.

The pickup had a bench seat, and on the drive home I sat next to Jimmy like a real country gal. We rolled down the windows and turned up the radio. I kissed his neck and the side of his face. I touched his chest, his arms, his downy hair. He kept his hand on my thigh. Twice he had to stop the truck, once for a lumbering possum, once for a pair of fat raccoons, but he shifted quickly into gear and put his hand back where it belonged. When we turned onto the county road, he parted my legs a little, his fingers firm but gentle, and then a little more, and he kept stroking lightly, teasing, until I was squirming and giggling and almost frantic, so I kicked off my sandals and wriggled out of my cutoffs and he kept his eyes intent and focused on the gravel road and his hand intent and focused on me and we kept on like that, ramping it up, until we finally turned onto the lane and reached the house and the truck lurched as he slammed it into park and we fell on each other, laughing because we were acting like teenagers—we were necking in the car! We were *parking* right outside the house where we lived because we couldn't wait, we couldn't wait—and he pulled me gently by the wrist and I felt the cool sandy dirt under the soles of my feet and the night air on my arms and I took off my shirt so I could feel that air everywhere and he kissed bare skin, breasts, chest, neck, mouth, shoulders, and I unbuttoned his Levis and leaned against the truck, helpless now, surrendering utterly, *take me*, I thought, *I want to be taken*, and then he said—he whispered—"Stand just like that, Thea." Stand just like that. And I did. I didn't move. I stood just like that. And he—he slowed everything down. I was gasping now, trembling, and we kept eyes open, eyes looking into each other's eyes so we could see what happened the moment he entered me, which he did, slowly, and then there was no more laughter, just the soft repeating of each other's names amid the oh my Gods and the animal sounds we were making amid the other nighttime animal sounds, the cicadas and the crickets and the owl in his pen and the coyotes yipping and howling at each other across the hills, across some unknowable distance, but we didn't hear any of that or heard it only faintly because we were the only two living beings on the planet, and we weren't stopping until we were done, we could do this all night if we wanted, we would do it all night, you bet we would, we were fucking like there was no tomorrow and there was no tomorrow, there was only *this*, now, yes, more.

Yeah. I wasn't going anywhere.

PART II

Home is where I want to be

But I guess I'm already there

—Talking Heads, "This Must Be the Place (Naive Melody)"

FIGHT, FLIGHT, OR FREEZE

THE FRIENDS JIMMY INVITED to the solstice party were people he'd known for years. I couldn't imagine keeping up with so many people from high school and college. I didn't have that many friends in high school and college. I had boyfriends, and I had Emily, and a few fellow theater majors I'd grown close to, people I promised to stay in touch with, but in a few years—months even, or another week, or ten minutes—we wouldn't know each other's current addresses. I was daunted by Jimmy's tight network. All these people, keeping tabs on you, coming to your rescue, bringing bowls of potato salad to your house. All that history. I worried about whether I would fit in with his clan, or if I even wanted to. A Tornado Hill–sized mound of stuff that I didn't know about loomed.

On the morning of the party, Jimmy went to town for beer and last-minute groceries. The elm and mulberry trees in the yard shaded the house most of the day. I sat on the deck shucking corn. I hadn't shucked corn in a long time. Emily and I must have done it in New Hampshire, but what I remembered was sitting on the patio in the Hudson Valley house, my mother chattering next to me, giving me the sticky silk to play with.

The hills and open fields brought to mind old social studies textbook descriptions of the early settlers, those intrepid people in their covered wagons, their *Little House on the Prairie* bonnets with the strings hanging down, and I could easily picture how they might have stopped in this very spot for the night to make a fire and cook whatever they ate back then (squirrel? woodchuck? snake?) and sleep under the expansive sky. I looked at the cottonwood trees and the rolling hills and fields and ignored the telephone poles and wires, trying to imagine what those explorers must have felt. Before I could get very far with that line of thought, a car turned onto the lane and made its bumpy approach to the house.

The driver, who could see me—see someone—on the porch, took the potholes hesitantly, as if to say, "Hmmm, who could that be?" When the car got close enough for me to see through the windshield, my heart performed two maneuvers simultaneously: Sank. Raced.

Amira.

She pulled into the spot next to Jimmy's and got out of the car. Josie, who'd been napping at my feet, woke up and took one look and started up with the barking routine. I put her in the house, where she whined and growled for another minute.

Amira carried a large tapestry bag with leather loop handles, impractical but striking. She dug inside it as she walked up the stone path. Then she looked up, as if just noticing me. "Well, well, fancy meeting you here." She smiled. I could tell she couldn't remember my name.

"Thea," I said.

"Ah, right." She found her pack of cigarettes and a lighter and lit up. "Weren't you supposed to be somewhere else by now?" I looked around as if the right thing to say would come to me, but she put up her hand. "That's okay. I don't need to hear the gory details. So—is Jamie here? Or has he left you to do all the work?" She indicated the ears of corn.

Jamie. "He's getting the keg. He should be back soon." I felt like the dog walker or the house sitter relaying a phone message.

"Good. I'll put my things inside, then we can catch up." She shifted her long black hair in a Cher move. She started to open the door, but Josie picked up where she had left off. "You still have that dog, I see."

I apologized and stuck Josie in the laundry room, then took the corn husks to the compost heap behind the barn. By the time I returned, Amira was sitting in the rocker, my favorite chair. She had changed from jeans into a black muslin skirt, ankle length, and a lime-green tank top that revealed a sprinkling of moles on her pale chest and neck. I remembered the hair on her back. Her feet were bare, toenails painted a deep purple.

Her eyes—and half her face—were hidden behind large sunglasses. I glanced toward the road, hoping to see Jimmy's truck.

She lit another cigarette and commented on the state of the vegetable garden. Jamie had planted broccoli and cauliflower in March, she said, but the wet spring had delayed the harvest. "Looks like he still hasn't repainted the barn. He was going to do it before the weather gets too hot." She noted a few other changes in the property. I made assenting sounds. Then she put out the half-finished cigarette in the bucket of sand Jimmy kept on the deck for that purpose. "Well, Thea"—she pronounced it correctly this time—"we might as well get to work."

I brought the big pot of corn inside. She started removing food from the fridge. "So what's his menu? Coleslaw? Ratatouille? Corn bread? He's doing pork ribs, not chicken, right?"

"Pork and beef."

"Has he done the sauce yet?"

"I—don't think he has."

"The ribs are better if you cook them in the oven and then let them marinate in the sauce all day before you grill them." She washed her hands and took a dish towel from the drawer, tucking it into the waistband of her skirt. "Would you get the ribs for me? I assume they're in the laundry room fridge. I'll chop the onions." She got out the wooden board and knife. Then she stepped over to the windowsill, picked up the tortoiseshell barrette, and clipped back her long hair.

~

I chopped eggplant and peppers under Amira's direction. She had warmed up to me, as if now that she had established her superiority, she could grant me entry into her domain. She asked what I thought of Merdale and whether I was taking the summer off ("lady of leisure" was the phrase she used) and I told her about my job at Julie's store. She raised her eyebrows and murmured something about the used book business.

Finally Jimmy arrived. He honked the horn twice to let me know he was home. I opened the door for him—his hands were full—and he gave me a quick kiss. I took the grocery bags and set them on the counter.

Amira moved in for a hug that struck me as a few beats too long. Jimmy and I exchanged a glance over her shoulder, but I couldn't read what he was telling me. Amira's mood transformed. She almost chirped her greetings. How glad she was to be back home in Kansas, she said, what a difficult trip it had been, the flight had been delayed, the weather was dreadfully hot and humid, and the *traffic* . . .

"So how's your dad?" Jimmy asked. He was unloading the bags and lining up items on the counter—tequila, triple sec, limes, crackers, cheese, bags of grapes.

"He's made an even bigger financial mess than I feared. But I got him squared away. The place is nice. Not the usual nursing home smell. There's even an aviary, where he can sit and watch the birds to his heart's content. He thinks he's on his back porch. We never had one, so I don't know what porch he's talking about."

"Amira's been in Florida," Jimmy said to me, "which is why you haven't met her until now."

I started to tell him that we had in fact met, but she interrupted.

"And now here we are, the two of us, slaving away together in your kitchen like old compadres." She winked at me. She was a good winker. I felt myself blush, stupidly pleased.

Jimmy opened the oven door. "Amira, I was going to put the ribs in the smoker."

"This'll be better, trust me."

"You're such a pain in the ass."

"I know. But you love me anyway." She vamped and lit another cigarette and asked me to pass her an ashtray. She talked to Jimmy about putting her father's house on the market, and the tree limb that had fallen onto his roof, and his worsening dementia. Just as I had begun to feel almost invisible, she gestured toward me with her chin. "So, I like your new friend."

"I like her, too."

"I'll bet." She smiled. "He always goes for the skinny girls," she said to me. Jimmy shot her a look. Was I skinny? I was thin, but skinny had a different, less attractive connotation. I hadn't ever thought of myself as skinny. And who else had been skinny? Was there a specific skinny girl

Amira was referring to, a recent one? I pictured a thin line of thin girls, parading down the lane, all jutting hip bones and shoulder blades.

Amira was not skinny. She was solid and strong. She began slicing limes so fast I worried there'd be blood. Her tank top showed off her toned arms and broad shoulders. She probably belonged to a gym. I touched my own bicep, or lack thereof. Maybe I should start working out. I hadn't thought about exercise in what seemed like a very long time. She opened a bottom cabinet and took out a juicer. Those limes didn't stand a chance.

Jimmy asked me to give him a hand outside. I tried not to appear too eager to escape. We unloaded the ice and the keg and carted coolers from the barn.

"How do you and Amira know each other?"

"Amira? She's from the old days. We met in college, and then we were in grad school together. Well, I was in grad school, she was in law school." We wiped the barn dust off the coolers with rags. "Everyone is from the old days. Except you. You're from the new days." He kissed me.

I told him about meeting Amira at Wendy's, and how Josie had nipped her hand, which made him laugh. "Josie? That sweetheart?"

"I know. She doesn't react to anyone else like that."

Jimmy cut the bags of ice open with a pocketknife, and we arranged alternating layers of ice and bottles. "Amira can be intimidating. She enjoys the occasional . . . confrontation. It's what makes her a good lawyer. Plus she provides her services to friends for cheap."

"Everyone needs a good attorney, I always say." I had never said that. I'd never needed an attorney. Why would you need an attorney, unless you were in trouble?

"She does some pretty cool pro bono work, with kids who are heading down the juvie-hall path." He dumped the last of the ice. "She's harmless. She's just good at being in charge. It's what she likes best."

"I like being with you best," I said. I felt clingy and pathetic, worried about Jimmy's friends judging me and finding me lacking.

"You're the sweetest girl." He kissed me again and glanced at the truck and then back at me, and we smiled, recalling the night before, the drive home and the dark night and the two of us mad for each other.

But I didn't feel sweet. I felt small and greedy. I wanted Jimmy all to myself. He went back to the barn for lawn chairs. I sensed Amira in the kitchen, watching us from the window. I didn't turn to see if I was right. I just wished she would go away, and everyone else, too.

~

As soon as Rocky arrived, Jimmy went into host-mode. I felt lonesome for the other Jimmy, my Jimmy. He introduced Rocky as a country doctor. I thought he was kidding at first. Rocky—Ray Rococco—did not look like a doctor, country or otherwise. He was wearing a blue bandana over his shaved head, pirate-style, a pair of wire-rimmed glasses, and a tight army-green T-shirt that showed off his buff upper body. We sat on the deck drinking keg beer in red plastic cups. Amira perched in the rocking chair and gazed at the fields. She seemed to be thinking of something else, as if she'd already heard everything that everyone had to say a hundred times. When Jimmy asked Rocky how things were going at the clinic, she sighed with impatience. The men ignored her.

"Funny you should ask." Rocky held a pouch of tobacco and some rolling papers in his lap. Doctors smoke, too, as it turns out. "Our old friend Ketchikan Larson came by this morning."

"How is Ketchikan?" Ketchikan was clearly an anecdotal mainstay.

"Ketchikan was having a little trouble breathing. So I examined him and found three broken ribs and a collapsed lung." Rocky had taken a slip of paper from the packet and tapped tobacco into the crease, and now he rolled the paper between thumbs and index fingers, licked the edge with the tip of his tongue, and sealed it. He performed this ritual as if we'd paid to watch. "So I said, 'Ketchikan, what happened? Were you in a car wreck? Did you fall down the stairs?' Ketchikan thinks for a minute, and then he says, 'Well gee, Doc, now that you mention it, my horse threw me a few days ago, and I lit right on my back. Hurt like the devil.'" Rocky laughed and lit the cigarette, exhaling smoke from his nose. "That tough old man had walked around with a flail chest for nearly a week. The pain alone would kill most people."

He told a few more stories featuring the heartiness of the farmers and ranchers in his practice, and we marveled on cue. Then he turned to me, as if only now registering my presence. "You'll have to excuse me," he said. "I was raised by wolves. Wolves and heathens. So where are you from, Thea?" But that was and wasn't his question. It was more like, So, where'd *you* come from?

"Thea is Wendy's niece," Jimmy said.

Amira added, "Thea was on her way back east, but got sidetracked."

"That happens," Rocky said.

I said I'd just graduated from college, and he raised his eyebrows in a way that made me wish I'd said something else, like *I've been crewing for a crabbing boat on the Bering Sea,* or *Maximum security wasn't as bad as I expected.* He asked me about Santa Cruz and the best surfing beaches, and I was able to answer him in some detail, thanks to Danny. As soon as Amira could get a word in she started peppering Jimmy with questions about his summer class syllabus and whether such-and-such former student/stalker had enrolled as he'd feared and if the window unit air conditioner in his office was finally working. I get it, I wanted to say. You can stop now.

Then Sylvia arrived. Rocky said, "Hey, sugar," and introduced her to me as his hot date, but Jimmy later told me they'd been living together for two years. She was the drummer in a girl band. She had spiky hair, purple and pink at the ends, and wore a short leather skirt and boots in spite of the warm weather. She had stubby thumbs—clubbed thumbs, I think they're called. Rocky and Sylvia seemed like the kind of couple who scream at each other and throw coffee mugs and ashtrays against the wall, then work it all out in bed.

Three guys arrived in a VW Rabbit, unfolding their long legs and stretching. They looked alike, and I couldn't keep their names straight. Then Nick and Julie, and Erika and George. Another four or five cars parked at the edge of the field, and suddenly there was a crowd. I didn't bother trying to meet everyone. I just smiled and said hi, and they did the same. All night long people came and went. Sometimes there were as many as forty, then we'd dwindle to half that, then another group would arrive or return, plastic-ringed six-packs dangling from fingers. One guy brought a six-pack of chocolate pudding snacks instead. "Fred's in AA," Julie explained.

I hung out on the porch with Lori, Gigi, and Julie. Josie lay shamelessly on Gigi's lap, though she was too big to be a lapdog. She had temporarily gotten over her animosity toward Amira when Amira paid her off in rib bones, but she still growled at her now and then, which made Amira laugh. Everyone was friendly and talking and drinking, and Amira kept carting things from the kitchen—pitchers of margaritas, chips and salsa, then a bowl of guacamole, then hummus and pita bread, then grapes and cheese—and people gushed their gratitude. She did a funny elaborate curtsy and went back inside for napkins. I started to ask if she needed help, but the door shut before she could hear me.

"Don't worry, she'll put you to work when she's ready," Gigi said, and Lori smiled.

I drank a margarita too quickly, trying to feel at ease. People were nice, but I could tell they were curbing themselves from asking too many questions. Why are you here? What are your intentions? When are you going home? And they did ask me questions, though less pointed ones. Where did you come from? What do you do? Where are you headed?

On the other hand, the evening was lovely. The air, the trees, the fields, the hills, the changing sky. I sat on the porch by Gigi's feet. Gigi was an art teacher at the high school in Merdale. She wore a leg brace and walked with a cane. I could see the metal part of the brace that attached to her shoe. Her drawstring pants were loose and baggy, so you couldn't tell where the brace began. I wondered whether she'd had an accident, or been born with some deformity. She kept Josie hypnotized by steadily stroking her nose. The dog was limp, zoned out, gone. Seeing my dog like that relaxed me.

Lori looked like a 1940s pinup girl, squashed. A squat torso and short legs, but these fine horizontal feline features, and thick blond hair, and breasts whose size you couldn't overlook. "I'm seriously thinking about a reduction," she said at one point, then apologized to Julie, who made a joke about how she'd take what Lori didn't want. Julie hadn't told me her story, just that she'd been in remission for three years. "Have babies," she'd advised me. "Have them while you're young. Have several. That'll help. It's all about the estrogen."

Lori was working as a secretary for an architect while finishing her BA. "I got waylaid," she said. "That 'year off' stretched into six." We talked about life post-college, how things never go as planned, Plan A and Plan B and Plan F, "as in Fucked." Gigi and Lori both laughed. But they were, they agreed, relatively content with their circumstances. They tried to convince me I had plenty of time to decide about the next step, but their stories seemed like direct evidence to the contrary. I needed to hurry up and commit to something before too much time elapsed.

"This is a good place to land," Lori said, nodding and smiling in Jimmy's direction. He and the three VW guys were setting up the badminton net.

Gigi nudged Lori with her good leg. "Leave it alone, Lorelai. It's none of our beeswax." I pretended not to hear.

A little while later, Jimmy offered us rackets to join the game in progress, but we lazily demurred. I found myself perking up when he was around, willing him to do something that would prove to everyone how much he liked me. I was worried that people assumed our shacking up (Sylvia's phrase: "you and Jimmy shacking up?") was all my idea, that I had pushed myself on the laid-back Jimmy, a freeloading drifter he couldn't get rid of. When he stepped on to the deck and placed his hand momentarily on my short-haired head like a blessing, I smiled. I wanted to rub against his leg like a cat.

I kept thinking I should help Jimmy at the grill, or Amira in the kitchen, or at least show her I knew where the forks were kept, drink from my gray-blue mug, stake out some territory—but I liked these women and their stories and their equanimity, and I didn't want to move. Then Bob and Wendy pulled up, and I was glad they'd arrived, that people would see Wendy embrace me and claim me as hers. I touched my fingertip to my forehead as if I could still feel the kiss she had placed there.

"You're just in time for dinner," Jimmy called out.

"Sorry we're late, James," Wendy said. By the looks of the two of them, they were in the middle of a fight, though Bob seemed unperturbed as usual. She was wearing a white T-shirt that said RIDE SALLY RIDE and carrying a bowl of cut melon, ranting about how clueless Bob was. "We've got our first American woman up in *space*," she sputtered. "Even as we stand here, she's up there"—she pointed emphatically to the sky—"and all *he* can do is crack dumb jokes."

"I was just wondering how she's going to pee."

"It's like living with a caveman. You think he'd be more evolved, what with his worldly travels. Were you even aware of the shuttle launch?"

She rattled off a few other news items, something about Nicaragua, and then a brief diatribe against Margaret Thatcher. She made a loud "tsk" sound, and took her bowl inside. Rocky and Nick broke into a chorus of "Mustang Sally." They improvised backup-singer moves, stepping from side to side, tapping one elbow and then the other, and we all laughed. "I hear you out there!" Wendy yelled through the screen door, to more laughter.

I realized I was clueless, too. I hadn't read a newspaper in what felt like months. The planet had been turning and turning. I felt as if I'd been having one of those dreams where you're falling, and you jolt awake. I should listen to NPR, I thought. I should find a *New York Times*. I should catch up. I went inside to join Wendy and see if Amira needed any last-minute help.

But she had done everything—cooked the corn, made corn bread, helped with Jimmy's coleslaw and ratatouille. She'd covered the table with a checkered tablecloth, set out the plates and silverware, cut some Queen Anne's lace and black-eyed Susans from the field and placed them in a vase. The food was lined up, buffet-style.

"Amira, everything looks wonderful," Julie said.

Jimmy herded everyone inside to get food, and loud, tipsy voices filled the room. I hung back with Amira, apologizing for not helping more. "That's okay," Amira said. "You can be the cleanup committee." She smiled, and I nodded back, even though I didn't want to be the cleanup committee. It didn't seem fair for me to be the entire cleanup committee.

Julie came over and pulled me by the hand. "Thea's first in line, our guest of honor." I started to object, but she pushed me gently ahead, and I took the plate she offered. I caught Jimmy's eye. He was watching and smiling.

George came into the house from the barn. He liked hanging out there. Too bad there weren't any other kids to play with. Sylvia had two children, but they stayed with her ex-Marine ex-husband in Minnesota every summer. George drifted over to Erika's side. He was shyer than when he'd been alone with us. Everyone was used to him and spoke to him kindly or else left him alone, since that was clearly his preference. Erika, in her cowboy boots and denim miniskirt, looked too young to be his mother. She wore black-framed, ironically nerdy glasses, and her hennaed hair was shoulder length with faddish chunky bangs. She could be the older sister, or the cool aunt. But she acted the part, talking to her son in low tones, asking him what he wanted, putting food on his plate and nudging him along. Twelve years old, and he seemed unable to serve himself. He kept his head down, shuffling along as if shackled. Poor kid. Poor Erika.

We took our plates to the deck or lawn. The fireflies began to come out. I hadn't realized how hungry I was. I let the voices rise and fall around me as I ate. Wendy sat in the deck chair next to me, and I asked her if everything was okay.

"Sorry for making such a scene. It's just—Bob. Bob, Bob, Bob." She laughed a sharp laugh. Josie, hoping for tidbits to fall from plates, stood on her hind legs. Wendy tossed her a bit of meat.

"So what happened? Was it really about the shuttle?"

"He's an idiot, that's what happened. He's an idiot, but I love him."

"So, the Sandinistas . . . ?" I chewed on a rib bone.

"I'm thirty-two years old. I want a baby, goddamn it. I want one with him. If he's not going to give me any, then I should leave. Only I don't want to leave. See? Either way I lose."

"Oh, Wendy, I'm sorry."

"And the thing is, what are we doing that's so important? What are we doing that would get in the way of babies?"

A burst of hilarity followed. People were gathered around Bob, and everyone was laughing at something he had just said.

"This is what we're doing. Drinking and hanging out and playing the clown." She put a piece of corn bread in her mouth. "Let's change the subject. How are you getting along? Everything okay with Jimmy?"

I assured her I was fine. I told her about the bookstore job, and how much I liked living in the country. She squinted at me, and I realized how I sounded—as if I planned on living there forever. I deflected and asked her about the college banquet. She'd had a better time than she expected. "Bob was so sweet. He bought me a corsage, like it was prom night or something." She smiled. "Oh, I almost forgot. Your mother called this morning. She said she didn't have 'your itinerary.' Haven't you been in touch with her?"

"Did she say why she was calling?"

"She just asked how you were doing. It didn't sound like an emergency or anything."

I sighed. "Wendy, it's my mother. It's always an emergency."

"I gave her Jimmy's number. I hope that's okay."

"Sure." Phoebe hadn't left her number, and she hadn't called me yet, so nothing was required of me.

I looked for the Tupperware container of brownies I'd taken out of the freezer earlier that day. Amira had tucked them away in a cabinet—a strange place to store brownies. The barrette, I noticed, was back on the windowsill. I took the brownies outside and passed them around.

～

After dinner, Jimmy and a team of assistants went behind the barn to finish the solstice project. A labyrinth of luminaries. He invited everyone to watch as the men fanned out and lit the tea light candles inside the bags. The geometric design unfolded in slow motion, a few magical lights at a time, like something being peeled back.

The group made appreciative noises and applauded.

"Don't catch on fire, Jimmy," the pudding guy said.

"Not funny," Nick said.

We were quiet for a moment. "It's so beautiful," Lori said.

Jimmy gave us each a candlestick, a book of matches, a slip of paper, and a pencil. "Write down a wish. Something for the coming year. It can be anything. But not, you know, world peace. The benevolent universe can only do so much. Then fold it up."

"Are we going to have to share?" Gigi asked.

"Only with the gods." He smiled at me. I couldn't tell if he was putting everyone on, or if he was sincere. A little of both, I decided.

People bent over their pieces of paper in the dark. Everyone, it seemed, knew what to ask for. Wendy was probably writing *Baby*. Julie, worried about the bookstore, would ask for brisker business. Nick, a carpentry contract; Bob, a grant to fund his wildlife projects; George, an end to his tics; Lori, her completed BA and a better job. I could see everyone else's desires but my own. I considered writing down *Make Jimmy fall in love with me*, but that sounded like a ninth grader pining over a crush. I glanced over at him now. He stood with hands in pockets, gazing up at the sky. I wondered what he had wished for, if he had wished at all.

My immediate need—another job to supplement my small paycheck—I could procure without divine intervention. And then it came to me. I wrote down one word.

Home.

The gods would, I trusted, know what to do with that.

We lit our candles and walked in a line toward the entrance of the labyrinth, led by Julie, whose sweet open face had gone as still and solemn as a priestess. Wendy was stationed at the entrance with a smudge stick, burning sage that she passed over each of us, starting at our feet and going up to our heads. Jimmy and I waited at the end of the line. "Amazing," I whispered.

"I read about these solstice rituals somewhere. I thought it'd be a lark." I smiled at his choice of words.

The summer darkness was thick and warm and soft. A fat orange moon had begun to rise in the sky. I focused on each step, and when we got to Wendy, she smiled at me and touched my shoulder. The sage smelled like pot, acrid and sweet and dense. The concentric paths intersected as they went around, so that the people ahead of you in line sometimes walked toward you, and sometimes away. Our feet swished against the grass. Someone tittered and was summarily shushed. What a spectacle we must have made—this line of thirty-odd supplicants snaking its way around flickering lights in the black field. Surely someone would drive by, assume something Satanic was going on, and call the sheriff. But no slowing headlights appeared on the road, and we continued our pilgrimage toward the center, strangely stirred. On the one hand, yes, it seemed contrived. But something else was going on, too, that primordial thing that happens whenever people assemble outside, at night, faces lit by firelight. I remembered the communal power of bonfires on the California beach, and camp-outs in the redwoods. Once, when the electricity went out at Spalding, a group of us gathered in the dining room with flashlights and spontaneously began telling our secrets, like ghost stories.

The clear space in the center held those who had finished walking the path. They stood in a loose circle, gazing at the candles they held. Jimmy and Wendy and I were the last to arrive. Jimmy whispered to Wendy, who nodded and stood in the center of the circle. She held up her piece of paper, then touched it to her candle's flame, watching it burn and letting it go just before it reached her fingertips. Julie burned her wish next, and everyone else followed, black ash floating into the still night like tiny wingless bats. Above, the sky was shot through with stars. Hey, Sally Ride, I thought. How do things look from up there?

Everyone looked at Jimmy, who just shrugged and said, "That's all I got, folks." But we wanted something else to happen. And that's when we saw Bob weaving his way toward the center. He hadn't walked the labyrinth with us. He was carrying something—a big black object on one arm.

"Eli," Jimmy said, smiling.

Bob wore the Darth Vader glove, the owl draped with a blanket. "I should take him out to the lake or somewhere. He'll probably just fly back to the pen. But it seems like the right time." He murmured something to the owl. Wendy stood next to him, her hand on her mouth. He lifted the blanket and raised his gloved arm, and the magnificent bird opened his healed wings and flew into the night. Everyone applauded.

And then we danced.

Music poured out of the house and onto the deck and lawn and the surrounding fields. The dancing was reckless, manic, lots of pogo jumping up and down. At one point I saw the badminton players carrying Gigi on their shoulders, a wreath of flowers on her head, and later a line of near-naked women—Sylvia, Erika, and Wendy—walked single file toward the pond, like the Three Graces. We all cheered and whistled at the sight.

At 1:00 a.m. I sat on the deck to rest. I had switched from margaritas to club soda, heading off a hangover, though I hoped that the dancing on the lawn and the kitchen cleanup (Nick and Julie had helped) would serve as preventative medicine. The party was smaller now. Bob and the badminton players and some other guys I hadn't met were on the deck swapping stories about their favorite concerts, Stones vs. Led Zeppelin, Springsteen vs. Clapton. Stevie Ray Vaughan's new album played on the stereo—"Love Struck Baby," "Pride and Joy"—and George was talking to Nick in an animated voice about Vaughan's tremolo picking style, his use of pentatonic blues scales. Nick didn't know anything about music. He was letting George teach him. Nick's attention was totally engaged, his listening a heartfelt, compassionate act.

Jimmy always said that music should make you want to drink, dance, and take off your clothes. He and Lori were still at it, Jimmy swinging Lori around and Lori shimmying and twirling, her shirt tied up around her large breasts, her feet bare. I waved at him, but he didn't see me. Then Amira appeared, carrying a tray of shot glasses filled with something red. "Nightcap time," she called. Jell-O shots. I hadn't done those since my freshman year of college. She distributed the shots then sat next to me.

"Here you go." She smiled and passed me the last glass on the tray. I didn't want a Jell-O shot. A Jell-O shot at that point in the evening seemed like a bad idea. But I didn't want to offend her. I lifted the glass in a toasting gesture and tossed it back. The cherry candy flavor bloomed in my mouth, then throat and stomach, then spread to my limbs, cool and warm at the same time.

Amira lit a cigarette. "Want one?" She drew another cigarette from her pack. I smoked only rarely. Okay, another peace offering, I thought. I lit the cigarette off hers, the hit of nicotine bringing me back to my first time—tenth grade, Emily and I sneaking behind the Art Building at Spalding. I felt fifteen again and pleasantly light-headed. I took another drag.

"So what do you think?" Amira asked. At first I thought she meant the cigarette, but she was referring to the scene at large.

"Is it always like this?"

"This is definitely a first. Who knows where he comes up with this stuff. On the one hand, he's tongue in cheek about it. He doesn't really believe in this shit. On the other hand, it's great, right? It's a great thing to do for everyone. People will tell the story later. 'Remember the wild solstice party out at Jamie's that time?' He throws a New Year's Eve party every year. The theme is 'don't have any expectations and you won't be disappointed.' But it's always a good time."

New Year's. I had a flash of kissing Jimmy at midnight. 1984! How bizarre. And all of these people would be there, drinking champagne and dancing and telling their stories.

In the dim light Amira's face looked lined and worn, but also serene. The pleasure of a job well done. This was her party, really, her success.

Hers and Jimmy's. They were partners in this production. And they were good at it. They'd mastered this particular art together. A perfect division of labor: Amira took care of everything inside the house (food, music, drinks), while Jimmy took care of everything outside (grilling, badminton, labyrinth). I wasn't jealous. I just felt the weight of their shared history. I understood how I must have seemed to her, dropping in out of nowhere, living with Jimmy. *What gives you the right?* I wanted to say something to her. I'm sorry if I'm messing things up for you. Maybe I shouldn't be here, but I can't be anywhere else right now. The thought of Eddie inevitably arose. I vowed I would call him the next day but also knew I wouldn't. I'd just keep putting my head in the sand—my favorite place to put it.

I thought about the women who had returned from the pond like sea nymphs with dripping hair and saw us all again in that candlelit circle, everyone with their private wishes, like children around a birthday cake. The funny thing was, as I reflected back, I couldn't remember Amira being there. I scanned over the faces in my mind—Wendy, Julie, Sylvia, Rocky, Carol, Gigi, Lori, the badminton boys ... the clusters of people whose names I didn't know ... George and Erika, standing next to Nick ... everyone except Amira. Where would she have been, if not with us? She was watching me now as if she could see these doubts playing across my face. I took another drag. I looked down at the cigarette. It felt like I'd been smoking it forever, but there was still half left. My arms appeared very long. And rubbery. I didn't think I could lift the cigarette to my lips again. I watched my hand as it reached forward to insert the butt meticulously into the bucket of sand. This seemed to take a long time. When I leaned back into the plastic weave of the lawn chair, I felt myself sinking, dissolving somehow, melding into the chair itself. I looked down at my legs, still solid but glimmering ominously. I wondered how I would stand up, and whether standing up was something I should try. I used all my remaining energy to keep my head from lolling forward.

Amira nodded in time to the song on the stereo. "Looks like old times," she said, indicating Jimmy and Lori. She exhaled smoke from her nose and meted out each word like tiny darts. "Back before Jamie and Vivian were married, he and Lori were quite the item."

Back before ... Jamie ... and Vivian ... were ... married ... I considered each word as if it were a stone I could turn over in my hands, examining its weight and size and geologic layers. Jamie, married? Wait. Jimmy? Married? I sank farther into the chair. Flight, fight, or freeze, I thought. The first two were impossible. I went for the third. I did my best to make my expression impassive, though I had no idea what my face looked like, or if I still had a face. I managed a sentence. The words seemed to come from somewhere behind me.

"Is ... that ... right ... ?"

Amira nodded, measuring my reaction with those dark eyes, then slowly turning her head back toward Jimmy, sphinxlike. "A lot of us have had our turn with Jamie. Now, I guess, it's yours. I wonder how long it'll last." After another bit of eternity she said something about sleeping bags and tents and went inside.

I turned my watery attention to Jimmy and Lori, who were going through all the old moves, the Swim, the Batman, the Twist, laughing at each other. It seemed cruel that he would do this in front of me. Lori wasn't the only one, either. As I sat immobilized, the invisible lines connecting Jimmy to each of the people at the party—and to many others I didn't know, would never know (*Vivian*? Would she make an appearance at some point, too? Was she at the party and I hadn't met her?)—became long silvery strands, tough as rope, forming an impenetrable net that would keep me out forever.

Of course, he didn't know about my friends and former lovers, either. Only no one was trying to trap *him* in the web of my past associations. As far as he was concerned, I was a free agent. No strings attached. He had accepted my appearance in his life, a young woman—a girl, really—who had materialized magically one afternoon as he stood in his vegetable patch and then, almost instantly it seemed to me now, moved into his bed. What a deal!

But all of this came to me in a thick haze, not as articulated thoughts. I wondered mildly if a dry ice machine was part of Jimmy's special effects show for the night. The gauzy world expanded and contracted with every inhalation and exhalation. I seemed to return to myself now and then, feeling a slam of awareness—as if I'd gone somewhere else, and now I was back.

Something was wrong. I felt the hard edge of panic and managed to stand up. I tried to find my sea legs. The seas were rough indeed. The boat, unseaworthy. The doorway when I reached it swooped and swayed, and I stepped inside the house, focusing on my feet so I wouldn't fall. Maybe I was sick. Food poisoning? Or the Jell-O had more than the usual shot? But I didn't feel drunk. I felt drugged. In and out like that. Here, then gone. I had to get upstairs. It seemed important that no one see me like this. I didn't want to embarrass Jimmy, or Wendy. Nobody else seemed similarly afflicted. They were going along as before.

"You feeling okay?" Amira said. She was sweeping the kitchen floor in long fluid strokes.

I murmured something that I hoped sounded like "fine." I would sleep it off. I waded through the thick air of the living room, where George was sacked out on the couch, and made the difficult, steep climb to the bedroom, using my hands to push myself from stair to stair.

Gone, then back again.

Now I was sitting on the floor. My suitcase was open in front of me. I'd taken it out of the closet. I guess I was checking on its whereabouts, or looking for something. Grains of sand had collected in the cracks—sand from the flip-flops I wore to the beach in Capitola, only a few weeks before. My ponytail was still in the side pocket. Time stretched out impossibly in all directions. Emily, I thought. Where are you right now? We'd always joked about her grass hut, but she would actually live in a one-room, concrete-block house, with an outdoor shower and cement floors that had drains in them, and mosquito netting over the narrow cot. Still I liked to think of her in the hut. She appeared before me now, a blurry apparition. She had that incredulous look.

He was married? And he didn't tell you?

She kept talking. I couldn't get all the words. Her tone changed. I listened more closely. *He seems like a good guy. You've only just met him. Stick around. See what happens.*

Pros. Cons.

For a few minutes I felt better. Maybe I was coming down from whatever I had taken. Then a velvety blackness started to creep into my peripheral vision like ink on tissue paper, spreading. The feeling wasn't entirely unpleasant. I found the bed and managed to climb onto it.

Emily spoke again, loudly this time, as if to shake me awake. *But, Thea*, she said. *Watch your back.*

~

And then—who knows how much later, maybe just five minutes, maybe as long as an hour—I felt a cold washcloth on my face. Someone spoke my name, over and over, and propped me up and gave me a drink of water.

"Wake up, Thea, wake up." I could smell Wendy's good beach smell, the soft hands stroking my head. I was sweating, I think, or chilled. Had I been crying? My throat felt constricted, my chest heavy. Wendy moved aside so Rocky could take my pulse. I looked around for Jimmy, who was standing at the end of the bed.

"I can't believe she did this," he was saying. He said it more than once. His arms were crossed over his chest, his face tense.

He was talking about Amira. I pieced together what I could from the conversation. She'd spiked some of the shots—barbiturates? hallucinogenics? both? She insisted they were just a party favor, a boost. The badminton boys loved them. Erika was furious—George found a leftover shot in the kitchen and thought it was dessert. She and Amira had a huge fight. Amira left. I'd missed a lot of drama. Rocky had monitored me and George, checking our pulses, our pupils. Is there a doctor in the house? There is.

Jimmy brought me a cup of tea. Everyone else went downstairs. He stayed with me, rubbing my back until I fell asleep.

~

I awoke the next morning with Jimmy lying next to me, his head resting on one arm. He was stroking my forehead with his fingertips, down the side of my face, along my neck. I thought of Gigi, petting Josie's nose.

"I'm so sorry, Thea," he said. "I can't believe this happened."

I cleared my throat. "Low tolerance," I managed. "Cheap date." I lifted my head to see how I felt. Woozy, fuzzy-brained, headachy, but overall intact. I had slept a deep dark sleep and remembered no dreams.

"Amira called to apologize. She says she feels terrible, she had no idea it would have such an effect on you. But I'm still pissed."

I felt like a child. George and I were the only ones who'd had adverse reactions. I was embarrassed that Jimmy's friends had seen me like this, that I'd failed to hold my liquor or my drug. Lightweight.

"Let's just forget it."

He looked down, then back at me. "I know you weren't in your right mind last night. But I have to ask you. Are you—are you thinking about leaving?"

I was confused. Did he want me to leave? "No. Why?"

"Your suitcase."

I looked over to where the opened suitcase still lay on the floor. "Oh. Ha. I think—I was looking for something. Emily's address." I twirled my finger next to my ear in the "cuckoo" sign.

"I just wanted to make sure you hadn't experienced, you know, some drug-induced revelation. Like, this guy's friends are nut jobs. I better get the hell out of here."

"They are nut jobs. But you can't get rid of me that easily."

"Good. I don't want you to leave."

"Good. Because I don't want to go."

He rolled onto his back. "And I don't want to cook breakfast for all these people."

"Is anyone awake yet?"

"It's only eight. They'll sleep for hours."

"Then let's go find a diner and get pancakes, and bacon, and French toast. And sausage. And coffee. And coffee cake." I was suddenly starving.

"But I have to be here when they wake up. They expect it. I'm the only one who knows how everyone likes their eggs."

I remembered Amira's pointed revelations about Jimmy. His past romance with Lori, his former marriage. That knowledge made me feel worse than whatever I had ingested in the Jell-O. But I decided to ignore it, for the time being. We would sort it out later. Right now I was just glad to have my faculties more or less in working order. I was glad to feel present in my body, in the room, in the world. And I wanted to feel the way I'd felt during these last couple of weeks, being with Jimmy, falling quickly in love.

I sat on top of him. He put his hands on my flat tummy, kissed it.

"It's my turn," I said. "And I want to drive into town and pretend we're on a road trip together and let these friends of yours take care of themselves. And I want to go now, before anybody wakes up."

"Just run away? Just like that?"

"Easiest thing in the world."

"Okay. But, first, do me a favor."

I smiled, happy to oblige this beautiful boy. "Anything," I said.

"Put away the suitcase."

So I did.

CHAPTER 7

SERIOUS THRILL ISSUES

A FEW LEFTOVER PARTY guests stayed till late afternoon on Sunday, drinking Bloody Marys and playing horseshoes, until Jimmy finally served them coffee and sent them home. We were cleaning up when the phone rang. It was Phoebe.

"Well, guess what," she said, as if we were in the middle of a conversation. "Your father's run off."

She was calling from Camden, Maine, where—in a bit of irony—she and Lyman were house-sitting for some friends for a couple of weeks. This house business was beginning to look like a game of musical chairs.

"Run off?"

"He left on some mysterious errand. I swear, it better not be that bimbo from Calgary again, because I've made it pretty darn clear—"

"Mother, he wouldn't carry on like that right under your nose." From what I could tell, both parents exaggerated the extent of my father's infidelities. Oh, I'm sure he fooled around. But mostly he was just a big flirt. He adored Phoebe. He knew how to clip the zone, creating just enough trouble to give her the drama she craved while not stepping too far over the line. Though admittedly, the divorces, however short-lived, suggested otherwise.

"He left a note on the kitchen counter saying he'd be gone for two days, but he didn't tell me why. I thought maybe he'd been in touch with you?"

Her voice dropped as if she were only now recognizing how unlikely this was.

"Haven't heard a peep."

Leaving a note on the kitchen counter was my parents' primary means of communication. Often the note was nearly illegible—they both had horrendous handwriting—or else they'd neglected to include the crucial details, like where the person was or when he or she might return. *Had to run!* was a favorite. *Chuck called, so I'll check in after a while.* You'd have no idea who "Chuck" was, or what "after a while" meant in human years.

"I hope he's not buying that boat. We saw a little sailboat for sale. He knows how much I hate the water. I hope he's not off somewhere, test-driving the thing." Then she talked about their trip, extolling the camper's fancy features but conceding that luxuries like a bathtub and a king-size bed could soon feel like necessities again. "Where are you, anyway?" she asked. "Wendy was hazy on the details."

An excellent student of my parents' equivocation techniques, I replied, "I'm sharing a house out in the country. You'd love it. I've got a gorgeous view." Outside Jimmy was continuing the post-party cleanup. We'd already disassembled the labyrinth, plucking luminary bags from the ground and tossing them into a wheelbarrow like turnips. Now he was collecting beer cans and bottles for recycling.

Phoebe acted as if she'd forgotten that my homelessness was, in part, her fault. But she hadn't forgotten. She just didn't want me mad at her. That was the real reason for her call. "You'll never guess who we bumped into," she said, hoping to charm me. She waited, but I didn't bite. "We were taking a stroll in Bar Harbor—remember Bar Harbor?—and there he was, that guy you used to go out with. What was his name?"

I rolled my eyes. "You'll need to narrow it down."

"Right, sorry, my daughter, the gal about town. He was very tall. This was at Spalding. I think Spalding. Or maybe the summer after you graduated. Anyway, he was at the marina, working as a fishing guide. He had his own boat, which your father was enamored with. Oh geez, I bet he *is* going to buy me that tamarind or whatever it's called."

"Catamaran."

"Right, whatever. The young man's boat was called *Serious Thrill Issues*. Isn't that so cute? What *was* his name?"

"Stephen? Stephen Lovejoy?"

"That's it! Stephen Lovejoy. How could I forget. And he specifically asked about you. What a coincidence that we would just happen to run into him, in Maine, while you're in Kansas of all places. You should be in touch with him. I have his address here, somewhere . . . I mean, his name *alone* . . ."

"Don't let that fool you, Mother. Stephen Lovejoy didn't provide much of either. He was just asking about me to be polite."

"Don't be so sure." My mother had theories about life that were drawn from dumbed-down versions of Jung. Synchronicity was her favorite. She was always looking for signs, connections, proof that there was order in her universe. Running into Lovejoy, a guy I worked with the summer I was twenty, had to mean something.

Then Lyman walked into the house, and exclamations ensued. I thought for a minute that Phoebe had forgotten me, but soon he came on the line. "Everything is fine, Dot." Hearing his voice brought unexpected tears to my eyes. He was the only one who called me Dot. Little Dot when I was little, or Polka Dot, Dotsie, Dottie, Dot-a-roo. "Pay no heed to the hysterics." Mother objected in the background, but he talked over her, apologizing again about the house, the sale happened so quickly, and he understood my nostalgia for the place but the time to sell was right. I was grown up, after all. I hadn't lived at home for years. All true enough.

I thought of the Gallaghers sitting around the dinner table. I remembered their affectionate teasing, the family lore, the fervent interest in each other's activities. They were playing roles, yes. But maybe that was better than nothing. Maybe that's just what families did for each other.

"I'm going to make it up to you," Lyman said. "You'll see. I love you, Dottie."

I sighed. "I love you, too, Daddy."

Phoebe got back on the phone. "A letter from Emily was forwarded with our other mail," she said. "I'll send it along. And just wait till you see the darling stamps. 'The Federated States of Micronesia,' with an exquisite white bird called a 'Sooty Tern.' That's what it says. Isn't that something? *Sooty tern.*"

I calculated the number of weeks since Emily left, trying to figure out how long it would take a letter from Eddie to reach her village. It didn't seem likely that she could have received reports of my delinquency and also had time to write me about it. Jimmy didn't have a mailbox at the house, just a PO box in Merdale. I gave my mother the address.

"Did I tell you? We may come for a visit later this summer. We're going to San Francisco. It's the twenty-fifth anniversary of when we met."

"I'll put it on my calendar." The likelihood of such a visit ever occurring was somewhere between nil and nil.

After we hung up, I stood at the window. Jimmy was messing around in the garden, picking zucchini and summer squash, weeding absentmindedly. He straightened and looked around for a minute or two. I remembered driving down the lane with Bob and seeing Jimmy for the first time, standing in that very spot, hoe in hand. Everything that had occurred in the interval, moving into his house and working at the bookstore and meeting this new cast of characters, seemed not quite real. *The plan was to deliver Emily's car to Eddie. The plan was to live at home. The plan was to sit in my backyard and read novels and reconnoiter and reconfigure the plan.* I had imagined that scenario so many times that it felt as if it had already happened or was happening somewhere else to some other self to whom I was tangentially connected, or maybe it was, somehow, still going to happen.

And then the house, sold. And then Eddie, concocting his own plan. And then me, looking out this window, at this man.

He saw me standing there and waved. I waved back. *Hello, whoever you are.*

I was drowsy and depressed. The drugs hadn't completely left my system. I went upstairs to lie down. Josie accompanied me, giving me worried sidelong glances before settling on her own bed and drifting off. Talking to my parents made me homesick. Not for them, or not just for them, but for my house. How I loved it there. How attached I was to that place. I'd always assumed I could go back anytime I wanted, forever and ever. Why had I assumed that? It was stupid. Of course my parents couldn't keep the house indefinitely. I tried my mental-tour trick, but picturing the empty quiet rooms only made me sadder. Worse, maybe they weren't empty and quiet. Maybe the new owners had already moved in with their furniture and appliances, their kids and pets and smells, their stupid plans to renovate and update.

It'll always be my house, I thought. Mine. They don't get to have it just because they live there.

I'd taken a healing arts class in college, because that's the kind of class they offered for elective credit at my groovy school, and I sat up to work on the *Letting Go* pressure points in my chest. I remembered the specifics of each step, though the math and science I'd allegedly learned were a dim memory. That stuff was just gone, the black holes their own black holes, sucking everything back into themselves as fast as they could. I applied pressure with my fingertips, then released pressure and tilted my head back, then reapplied pressure, and so on. I believed what they said about the body holding emotions, because touching these places above my lungs and heart released something in me, and before long I was crying. I curled up under the covers and succumbed. I was slipping into a dark well. Above me was the light, but I couldn't reach it. And the light faded. The aperture grew smaller. It might remain a pinpoint, or it might close up altogether.

When I heard Jimmy in the kitchen, I limped to the bathroom and turned on the shower, locking the door even though we never locked the door. I sat on the tub floor. I knew these hugged knees, this hot water on my back. I felt like there was a big knot I was trying to untangle, and once I figured out one end from the other, I could follow the rope to someplace that made sense. These episodes didn't happen often, but they happened enough for me to know the steps to take. Shower, nap, long walk, repeat. I would tell Jimmy I wasn't feeling well. In another day or two or three, the spell would lift, and I would emerge, blinking at the bright world, and return to the good people on the surface blithely going about their business.

HEDONICALLY ADAPTING

PROFESSOR PIERCE PIERSON'S HOUSE smelled of dog—even the front porch. He and his wife, Amanda, owned two decrepit Irish setters, Pinkie and Edna, one blind and one deaf. The dogs lay on the couches and beds, ate food off china plates, and shed their long red hair all over everything, including the professor in his wheelchair.

I'd found the ad on the Student Union bulletin board. Morning help needed: errands, research assistance (trips to the professor's departmental office to pick up his mail, Kinko's for photocopying, and occasional library legwork), light housekeeping. I interviewed before my bookstore shift on Monday and started work on Tuesday morning. At six dollars an hour the wage was nearly twice the minimum, and the professor paid me for four hours' work whether or not he needed me the whole time. Pierson was a psychology professor who had once been in private practice, and I hoped, after we got to know each other, that he might offer me some gratis advice, or even a full-blown therapy session or two.

As soon as I arrived in the morning, Amanda Pierson left to play tennis or golf. She was tall and angular with short salt-and-pepper hair and a businesslike manner. Actually, she was downright chilly, but I tried not to take it personally. I hadn't done anything to her, after all. She always acted as if I kept her waiting, when in truth I arrived five minutes early every day.

"Good morning, Mrs. Pierson," I said. She said a cursory hello, pointedly using my full name though I had told her that everyone called me Thea. She put her coffee cup in the sink, looked at her watch, and left.

"T-12, vertebral fracture," Pierce said to me on my first morning of work. "Hang gliding in Colorado, on a clear, sunny day. Everything was perfect, except for my gross miscalculations during takeoff. I'm a paraplegic, not a quad, which means no feeling from the waist down. It happened fourteen years ago. I've made my peace, such as it is, and I abhor pity, from myself or others." I nodded. He had given this speech before.

Meanwhile I took in the chaos around me. From the outside, the house was like the others on that street of faculty homes: solid, satisfied-looking structures built in the 1930s and '40s with front porches and detached single car garages. Maple and oak trees lined the street, and everyone in the neighborhood, except the Piersons, had flower beds out front. But the inside of the house was the real stunner. Dust balls skidded across the floor like tumbleweeds. The chrome trim around the sink and faucet was blackened with grime. Dark stains dotted the carpets and upholstery. You know those Lemon Fresh Pledge commercials, where the lady of the house wipes a cloth over a table and you can't believe anyone with a manicure like hers would ever allow her furniture to accumulate such a thick layer of dust? Well, that was the Pierson house. And not just dirt, but stacks of magazines, newspapers, and mail covering the kitchen and dining room tables. I itched to throw out everything in sight and take a scrub brush to the whole place.

A sitting room off the kitchen had been converted into the professor's office. A path wide enough for maneuvering his wheelchair was the only floor you could see. He wheeled back and forth between two desks, one on either side of the room. Crammed in the small space were bookshelves and filing cabinets, and more piles of file folders and manuscript pages and APA journals—some over a decade old. His wife had hung a curtain in the doorway to shield herself from the clutter, though the office wasn't much worse than the rest of the place. While she was gone, we tied the curtain back so he could enter and exit the room more easily. Mostly he stayed put.

I couldn't imagine what the "light housekeeping" in the ad referred to.

"I keep telling myself I'll get organized one of these days," he said. He was a handsome man in his fifties. Dapper, I thought. Cordial, well-groomed, *spruce*. He was writing a book on hedonic relativism. He gave me a mini-lecture on this concept, how human beings adapt to a certain level of material or other happiness and then recalibrate, perpetually yearning for the next, the better, thing.

"People are never satisfied," I agreed.

Pierce gave me a tight smile. "It's more complicated than that." I said something appeasing like, it's a fascinating subject, I'll look forward to learning more.

He outlined our routine. Every morning I was to stop on the way to work at Java Joe's, pick up coffee and a cranberry scone and his reserved copy of the *New York Times*, and let myself into the house. He would have a list of tasks ready so that I wouldn't break his concentration if he happened to be in the middle of a thought. "I'm not young, like you," he said. "Once an idea or sentence goes, it's gone." He expected me to stay in the kitchen or living room—within shouting distance—in case he needed me, though he emphasized that I would never be required to tend to his *person*. At eleven o'clock I could check to see if there was anything else needed that day. If not, I could walk the dogs, then leave. His aide arrived at noon, to make his lunch and tend to his physical care.

Except for the horrible house, the job was, at least initially, ideal. Easy but not boring, lots of variety, time spent at the library and in town, and good under-the-table pay. Often Pierce dismissed me early, and I had time to do my own errands before heading to Julie's bookstore. As always, I fell quickly and happily into my new routine. "Routine is your pal," Emily always said. "Stick with it." Maybe I was hedonically adapting, though. Once this routine got old, I'd start casting around for a new one.

The downside of the new job was that Jimmy and I had to give up our leisurely mornings in bed.

"Dr. Pierson?" Jimmy asked, when I described my first day on the job. "The guy in the wheelchair?"

"You know him?"

We were driving the ten miles home, past sights that were becoming familiar. There was the bottling plant, and the old bridge, and the river, the fried chicken restaurant, the used car lot, the abandoned roadside hotel, the horse farm, the trailer park. Then more farms and pastureland until we reached our turnoff. County road (gravel) for a few miles, dust swirling around the truck, Jimmy expertly avoiding each pothole and curve. I had my favorite vistas—an old barn, a field of yellow flowers, a limestone farmhouse—and felt pleased when I saw them, as if they were mine now.

"I've heard stories."

"Like what?"

"Just don't get too close to that wheelchair." He leered at me like the Big Bad Wolf. "The professor has grabby hands disease."

"Pierce Pierson?"

"Good news is, you can outrun him."

I couldn't imagine the professor getting fresh with me. He would be so embarrassed afterward, so horrified at his actions.

"He's a garden-variety lech. He always was. It's not the accident that did it. Just because he can't feel anything down there doesn't turn it off up here." He tapped his head.

I watched Pierson for signs that he had even a remote interest in me, but there was nothing. I dismissed Jimmy's story as mean-spirited campus gossip, or else old news. Maybe he had groped some undergraduates in his heyday, but the wheelchair changed all that. I felt sorry for him, living with his supercilious wife in that grungy house. He never seemed to leave it, either, though a ramp led to the front door, and presumably he got himself to campus during the school year to teach his classes and attend department meetings. Occasionally I peeked into his study, where he sat looking out the window. I'd wait until he picked up his pen again and began writing. More often than not he just sat, still as stone, all the time in the world to contemplate the ever-receding nature of happiness.

On my third or fourth day of work, I spilled some water on the speckled linoleum floor and wiped it up. The paper towel was black. The linoleum wasn't as speckled as I thought. I didn't have anything else to do at the moment, so I swept then mopped the floor with a sponge mop that crumbled into pieces from disuse and age. The professor called out, "You don't have to do that."

"I'm sorry, is the noise bothering you?"

"Not in the least. It's disgusting here, isn't it? Amanda abhors cleaning, but never gets around to hiring anyone. I'll pay you more for the housework."

"You don't have to," I said. "'Light housekeeping' was in the ad."

He smiled but didn't say anything else. I wiped down the counter and made a note to bring cleaning supplies. I'd leave them in my car until Amanda left. I didn't think she'd approve of me doing the housework, but she probably wouldn't stop me, either, as long we both pretended it wasn't happening. People were such a mystery. I couldn't begin to understand them.

~

Soon it was no longer a question of me interrupting the professor, but of him interrupting me. One morning I was in the study looking for a reference he needed. "So where in our pleasant city are you staying, Thea?" he asked. We had talked about my situation during the job interview. He knew I'd just graduated and that I had an aunt in town.

"With a friend," I answered, looking back at the folder in my lap. For a moment I worried he was going to offer me his guest room, though if there was a bed in there, you couldn't see it.

"Is this friend," he paused, "female? Or male?"

"Excuse me?"

"I'm sorry. Was that too personal?"

"I'm just trying to find that study on Self-Monitoring." Turns out there are high self-monitors and low self-monitors and I was definitely in the high group, watching my audience for cues and adjusting accordingly.

He was quiet for a moment, but then, unable to help himself, he continued. "I'm assuming male. You look like a woman newly in love." He wasn't flirting so much as trying to compliment me. Though maybe there's not much difference.

I put the folder down. "Professor Pierson."

He recoiled as if I had given him a light slap. "I'm so sorry. I didn't mean to offend."

"It's okay." Anything to make him stop sounding so pathetic. "It's just, my personal life is my own business."

"Of course. Forgive me. It won't happen again. You're an excellent assistant. I would hate to lose you because of an imprudent comment." He turned his chair back toward the window.

The last girl who worked for him left for Boston at the end of the spring semester. I felt that familiar stab of envy. Boston—*that's* what I should be doing. Now I wondered if she'd quit the job because of him. The whole thing was depressing. Here he was, trapped in this chair, this body, this house. No social life that I could tell—the calendar on the kitchen wall, which I'd had plenty of time to examine, tracked his wife's various activities and his medical appointments. He didn't seem to exist apart from the mess of his intellectual world. So what if he was rusty in the art of conversation? So what if he found talking to some twenty-two-year-old about her private life tantalizing?

I had hoped, too, though it seemed improbable now that I'd gotten to know him better, that the professor could help me. I played out conversations in my head. I wasn't especially interested in tracing the obvious *issues* back to my parents—who cared, really, that I had developed defense mechanisms or coping strategies or ways of compensating as a response to my pretty reasonable childhood? What I wanted was advice. I wanted someone to help me figure out where I should go, what I should do, who I should be. "Follow your passion," our commencement speaker had said. Excellent, if you know what your passion is. And you're *supposed* to know. It's your passion, after all. By definition it's intense and uncontrollable—not something you can ignore or forget or fail to recognize.

I put the folder down again with a sigh and spoke to the professor's back. "I'm living with someone I met when I came here, so things have developed fast. I really like him. We like each other. But I worry that, you know, I'm putting off my real life in some way. That I should be somewhere else, doing something else." The professor spun his chair in a half turn. The handsome planes of his face were more striking in profile. I waited for him to speak. Maybe I had divulged too much. Maybe he didn't want the details after all. "I guess it feels like I don't have very many options right now," I mumbled.

He looked at me. "Really? I'm guessing, Thea, that you have more options than you're allowing yourself to see." Then he rotated slowly back around and bent over his work.

RUNAWAY GIRLS

ON THE FOURTH OF July Jimmy and I were planning to watch the
Merdale fireworks display, which took place at the river, but that afternoon Bob and Rocky showed up with an injured fawn. A combine had
killed his mother and sibling and mangled one of his back legs. Rocky
gave him a dose of intravenous painkillers and performed a makeshift
surgery, then dressed and bandaged the wound. He didn't normally per-
form vet duties, but amputation, he said, was the same across species,
and the trip to the Merdale animal hospital would've taken too long.

The men set up a pen in the barn. Rocky said we would have to keep
an eye on the fawn for a couple days. I named him Hans and gave him
a bottle of milk spiked with antibiotics. I didn't care about missing the
fireworks. I already loved him, with his too-big ears and eyes, his spotted
fur, his bandaged stump. Bob could see the Bambi thing that was going
on with me and gave me emphatic instructions. No petting, no talking,
just the bottle. Rehabilitation and release. "You don't want him growing
up and getting all friendly with the asshole holding the rifle."

After they left I sat on the deck reading a book I'd borrowed from the
store. "Take all you want," Julie always said, motioning to the towers of
books. There were more piles in the storage room in the back that needed
to be priced and shelved, except we didn't have any shelf space left.

My new life had altered my reading habits. Usually, perhaps uncharac-
teristically, I liked to delve into one author or subject and stick with it for
a month or two. But that summer I read all over the place. Books about
etymology, gardening, abstract art. Biographies of famous Kansans—
Russell Stover, Amelia Earhart, Charlie Parker, Langston Hughes, Dwight

Eisenhower, Gwendolyn Brooks. Novels by Henry James, P. D. James, James Joyce, James Baldwin. I read fast, skimming or skipping large sections or entire chapters, as if searching for a clue. Sometimes I made a few notes on index cards, but I rarely bothered to write down the book title or author—the sources seemed so obvious to me at the time—and later, when I looked at these cards, they made no sense. Whatever had struck me as significant was meaningless out of context. The notes read like the babblings of a madwoman. That afternoon I was reading a book about a woman who traveled across the Australian desert with a camel. I didn't want to cross the desert with a camel. But I was so absorbed by her adventure, doing anything else seemed like a waste of time.

Jimmy joined me on the deck, carrying a .22 pistol that he used to shoot carpenter bees. He lined up the furry corpses at the edge of the deck, proud of the body count. "They drill holes right into the house," he said when I objected. The bees were the size of bing cherries, and Jimmy was right—you could see the holes they had made in the eaves.

Ever since the solstice party, I'd been waiting for him to mention Vivian. We hadn't shared much about our pasts. We hadn't ever had that dicey conversation that usually occurs early in the relationship. You tell me yours, I'll tell you mine, we'll offer up (usually damning) summaries of the affairs, then compare lists, implicitly or explicitly (how many? how serious? how recent?). We'd skipped all that. I guess we wanted to stay in the bubble of the present. And analyzing the past wasn't exactly Jimmy's thing anyway. Still, it struck me as odd that he had never said the words "my ex-wife" even in passing, even in reference to something else. Old girlfriends were one thing. Wives, I felt, were in the full-disclosure category. I even wondered if Amira had invented the whole story, serving it up as a lethal Jell-O shot chaser.

I put down my book and watched him aim at another swaying bee.

"Amira said something to me at the solstice party," I began. He shot and missed.

"Yeah?" He aimed again, squinting in a fetching manner. Shot at the bee. Hit it. Lined it up alongside the others, then turned his attention to me.

"She said something about you and Lori, being 'an item.'"

"Lori? Oh yeah, we were hot and heavy all right."

My heart sank. I thought of them dancing and wondered how often I'd have to endure seeing them together.

Jimmy laughed when he saw my face. "Honey, Lori and Gigi have been together for three years. I was one of her experiments with men. It didn't go so well."

I clapped my hand to my mouth. "I'm such an idiot."

"Amira likes to stir the pot. It's her least attractive quality." He scanned the area for more bees.

"She also mentioned . . . Vivian." I didn't look at him when I said her name.

He turned toward the road, as if he were expecting someone. His shoulders dropped in a way that made me regret saying the name. "What did she say about Vivian?"

"Just that you two were married."

"I swear, Amira can be such a pain in the ass sometimes."

"I think she wanted to make me—uncomfortable."

"She's possessive. She wants this little world out here to be a closed circle."

I thought of the barrette. "She wants you all to herself." He shook his head. But when I said it, I knew I was right.

"She just hates change. She has her ideas about how things should be."

"Does she always behave this way—around your new girlfriends?" I felt presumptuous. We hadn't ever said "girlfriend," "boyfriend." Those words seemed silly anyway, high school stuff. But what else could we call each other? A few years before, the Census Bureau had come up with a stupid acronym—POSSLQ. *Person of Opposite Sex Sharing Living Quarters.* What did the Bureau do with Lori and Gigi? Probably there was a euphemism to check, "roommates" or "companions."

Jimmy examined the pistol, put the safety on, and sat down next to me. "It's been a while since Amira has met anyone I've dated. For one thing, I haven't actually *dated* much in the past couple of years. Nothing serious, anyway. And for another, since building the new house I've tried to keep some distance from the old life. Though the old life does have a way of showing up here to party whenever it wants." He was right. Every other day, it seemed, people came out to the house, often dropping by without calling—friends from college or graduate school, former students, old drinking buddies. Jimmy always seemed game. He put the speakers in the windows and turned up the music, fired up the grill, put up the badminton net, made beer runs. Sometimes I went to bed before the party was over and in the morning awoke to find tents pitched on the front lawn. Truth is, I was growing tired of all those people hanging around all the time. I was tired of being the cleanup committee. The one saving grace was that Amira had been scarce, busy with a trial in Topeka.

"It's hard to keep *me* separate, though, since I'm always here." I was careful not to say *living* here.

He lay the pistol on the deck next to his chair and held my hand. "I'm glad you're here. It's none of Amira's business, who I'm with. And if you were living in town, I'd want you to stay with me every minute I could. You would've been here for the party, and Amira would've said what she said to you regardless."

I nodded. "I'd want to be here every minute, too."

"Good. Then there's no problem." He kissed my palm and gave me my hand back, done with the conversation.

"But I want to know about you. I want to know about your life before me."

He laughed, but there was an edge to it. "Girls. Why do girls always want to know the old stories? Thea, the Vivian story is a bad story. I don't talk about Vivian because my time with her was—difficult. A marriage that happened too young and that should never have happened at all."

"Oh."

"And you want to hear about it anyway." He was frowning, eyes on his hands.

"With a lead-in like that ..." I was trying to keep the conversation light. I didn't want to wreck the pleasant evening, but a fraught mood had already descended. For a moment I almost said, You know what? Let's forget about it. Let's just pretend we have no pasts—we're young, after all! How bad can the past be? Let's go for a walk, play Scrabble, have a beer, check the garden for stealth zucchini. (They grew to the size of femurs overnight.) We'll talk about it another day.

But from the look on Jimmy's face I could see I had already popped the bubble. And anyway, he was never going to speak about Vivian unless I pushed him. I couldn't live with him and remain in the dark about his marriage. If Amira hadn't said anything, surely someone else would've mentioned Vivian. How does an ex-wife not come up in conversation? Wendy hadn't told me about Vivian, but then again, Wendy had only met Jimmy a year ago.

He put his head back and shut his eyes, as if trying to imagine where to begin. "I told you about Amira's little side interest, right? How she works with juvenile delinquents and wayward girls." He glanced at me, checking for a reaction, but I had no idea where he was headed. He took a deep breath. "Vivian was, at one time, one of Amira's runaways." I concentrated on keeping my face neutral. I would not judge him for this. Still, *runaway* was not what I had expected. I folded my hands over my stomach. "Just for the record, I didn't know that until much later. Though Vivian did tell me stories about her nightmare of a childhood—seven foster homes, poverty, abuse by various authority figures. Eventually she got picked up for shoplifting, then breaking and entering. Amira kept her out of jail. She found her a group home and a job, took her to counseling." We watched another carpenter bee make its drunken way toward the eaves, but Jimmy made no move for his gun. "Amira had this weird sisterly bond with Vivian. I never figured it out. But their relationship was different from her other cases."

"So Amira introduced the two of you?" I couldn't imagine how such an introduction would work. Hey, Jamie, there's this cute little felon I'd like you to meet?

"She had a bunch of people over for dinner. That was the first time I saw Vivian. I drank too much and ended up spending the night. I didn't see her again for almost a year. And then Amira brought her out here for the weekend. Well, not here—the old house." Vivian was working in the office of a steel and pipe supply company and had her own apartment, he said. She was more or less on her feet. She seemed more solid, independent, capable.

Jimmy was twenty-four or twenty-five by then. He'd inherited the house from his grandparents. He was commuting an hour to graduate school a few times a week and working on the house, which was a shambles. No one had lived in it for a decade except mice. Vivian, he said, fell in love with the place. She had romantic notions about the country, getting back to nature, all that. She started coming out to visit on her own. She didn't have a car, so she hitchhiked.

"And so you guys were . . . ?"

"We weren't all that serious. She'd talk about these other guys she was seeing in Topeka, and I figured I was just part of the weekend getaway package."

I shifted in my seat. Did he see me in the same way? Romantic about the country, looking for a summer getaway package? Maybe I was those things.

"One Sunday afternoon, when she was supposed to go home, she started crying. She hated her life, she didn't want to leave, she loved me, she loved the house. She stayed here for a week. I kept telling her to call in sick at work, but she didn't. She *wanted* to lose her job and her apartment so she'd have nowhere else to go. I probably should've put a stop to it. But Vivian was—she was hard to ignore."

Beautiful? I wanted to ask. But I didn't really want to know.

"She was so damaged and fragile, but also tough. A survivor. She still is, no doubt. She was young, but she had this old soul. And she had this scary, attractive energy. Like she'd do anything. She'd look at me sometimes, and I'd think—stay back. But I didn't. Part of me was deeply, stupidly in love with her."

Naturally if he married her, he was in love with her. But I didn't want to hear *deeply*.

"I didn't get, at first, how troubled she was. And not only because of her history. She was just so intense. She could be almost violent, throwing things, screaming." He had attributed her behavior to passion— their passion for each other. "I look back now, and it's clear there was something wrong with her. She needed help. Medication. A straitjacket. Something." He rubbed his hand over his face. Things between them would go smoothly for a period of time, and he'd convince himself their relationship was solid. They worked on the house together. She was a hard worker, often staying up all night to finish a project. She got a job at a horse farm nearby. Life went along fine for a while, and he thought everything might work out.

"So," he threw up his hands, "we got married. Her idea. We just went to the courthouse one afternoon and signed the papers."

I could see Jimmy on the steps of the limestone courthouse in Merdale, kissing Vivian and smiling. I imagined a willowy girl in a tea-length antique lace dress, daisies in her hair.

They were married a couple of years, "give or take." Then, Jimmy said, she met a guy named Ryan. He was a minister. She had never been religious, but she started going to Ryan's church, spending more and more time with him. "I was busy, working on my dissertation and teaching, it was a crazy time, and I knew she was lonely. I thought maybe Ryan could help her find some equilibrium. But she was spending more and more time with him, less and less time at home. I tried to talk to her about it. I don't know. I probably didn't try very hard."

Vivian began to talk about her calling. How God had a larger purpose in mind for her. She'd never been to church before, never talked about anything remotely spiritual, at least not to Jimmy. But here she was, a believer. One day he came home and she was sitting at the kitchen table, hands folded, waiting for him. She announced that Ryan was going on a missionary trip to South America. He was helping to start a school there, and she wanted to go with him. She believed they were fated to be together and bring the message of God's love to the world.

"Even then I thought she meant that she would go and come back. But that's not what she meant."

"She wanted a divorce."

"That's not the worst of it."

"What? What happened?"

"She left the night the old house burned down." Jimmy gave me a level look. "Amira thinks that Vivian set it. She was so furious at me—"

"Vivian was furious at *you*?"

"She said I was too passive, I should be fighting for her, I shouldn't let her go so easily. I said who was I to fight with *God*? But she knew I didn't take much stock in the whole God thing. She knew I was relieved to be off the hook. Part of me was relieved. And it's not like she wanted to stay here. She just wanted me to want her to stay."

I tried to take all this in. "So you're saying, Vivian was leaving you, and was angry that you were letting her go, and she set your house on fire."

"I was never convinced of that," he said. The house was so old, and the wood termite-infested—almost anything could have started it. He knew the danger. He'd kept fire extinguishers in every room. I took Jimmy's hand, but he just squeezed it once and let go, as if he had to plow ahead without me.

"The night she left, several of us were partying up at the pond. I wanted a buffer, you know? George was here, too. He had his own tent. He loved that tent. He used to pitch it next to the barn, and he'd use his walkie-talkies when he needed something. Then the freaking house burns down. He had problems before, but he got worse after that."

"I'm so sorry." I wanted to touch his arm, his face, but he had shifted away from me, occupying a separate space.

"Who knows? Maybe Vivian leaving and the fire starting was just a wild coincidence. Maybe the two had nothing whatsoever to do with each other. Or maybe she lit a candle near a curtain, just for the hell of it. She always loved a dramatic exit."

He lost everything in the fire. He used to be a pack rat. He'd saved photos, stamp collections, Boy Scout merit badges, birthday cards from grandparents. The month before, he'd taken all his stuff from his parents' house. They were moving to a condo in Arizona and didn't have room to store his old board games, lab notes from high school chemistry, World Book encyclopedias. "I lost my dissertation, too. I'd made a copy, but both the copy and the original were in the house. I was one chapter short of finishing. After that, I was sort of done, you know? Done with the PhD, done with saving things. I travel light, now. I got the message." He smiled, speaking in a phony, inflated voice. "It's all impermanence. Easy come, easy go."

I asked about the divorce. Amira had filed the papers before Vivian left. Only one party has to appear in court. Jimmy took care of the last details, and Vivian ran off to her Chilean village. "She didn't leave me an address. I wasn't exactly interested in corresponding anyway. End of story."

I'd been sitting tensely forward in my chair, not moving. I sat back and breathed. Dark shadows had appeared under Jimmy's eyes. He looked wrung out. Dusk had fallen, and the sky was streaked with pink and orange and lavender. A mosquito whined at my ear, and I brushed it away. Eddie once told me that a mosquito's irritating high-pitched drone was a kind of mating call. I waved at my ear again, shooing away the thought of Eddie. Sometimes he popped into my head at the most inopportune times.

I didn't ask anything else. I didn't mention Amira's comment about everyone having had a turn with Jimmy. I didn't want to know any more.

But part of me did want reciprocity. I wanted him to ask about my past. Maybe not at that exact moment, but sometime. I wanted to confess about Eddie. That secret was a burden. The longer Jimmy and I were together, the harder it was to come clean. Even when I was being honest with myself, instead of rationalizing away the truth with the usual excuses (*Eddie can't possibly think we're engaged, he's forgotten the whole episode by now or else wishes he could*), I couldn't figure out the context in which bringing up Eddie made sense.

And Jimmy didn't want to know. He didn't want to hear about where I'd come from, or my troubles in love. Vivian had cured him of curiosity regarding such matters. We walked to the barn to check on Hans. Jimmy put his arm around me, and I leaned into him gratefully. Forget Vivian, I thought. Forget Eddie. Forget everyone. In the distance, fireworks started to pop and crack like gunshot.

SOMETHING'S GOT TO GIVE

EMILY AND I AGREED that three things determine a job's worth: 1) You like the work itself. 2) You like the people you work with. 3) The money's good. Our rule was that you stick with any job that offers two out of three. At the professor's, I had the work and the money. At the bookstore, I had the work and the people. I'd had so many jobs where none of the three applied that I felt I was making huge strides in the career department. I'd been a waitress and a dishwasher, swept up hair and answered the phone in a hair salon, worked as a housekeeper at a Holiday Inn—that was the worst. I'd done brief stints in telemarketing and selling things door-to-door (Avon, vacuum cleaners, encyclopedias). In college I tutored a James Bond–obsessed tenth grader in French. I wrapped gifts at a department store, but I only lasted one day because my wrapping always looks like a little kid tried to do it, all bunchy and too much tape. I sold concessions at a summer stock theater where my father directed plays. I was a camp counselor for two weeks, but the camp closed down because of a meningitis outbreak. My senior year of college I was a clerk at a public library circulation desk—that was my favorite.

But now I had landed two jobs in which I was, sort of, using my college degree. The professor had discovered I could edit and proofread and paid me extra for these duties. I still hadn't found a "career path," but I'd landed two above-average gigs. Not bad, was my thinking.

Then the professor showed me the French maid costume.

He had continued bugging me about Jimmy, and he seemed to enjoy the inevitable verbal spanking I gave him. It became a kind of game, one I could play with little cost. Perhaps I was being sexually harassed. On the other hand, I didn't mind.

"How's my friend James these days?" he asked.

I looked up from the chapter I was proofreading about willpower and the development of a sense of self. Here was some information I should pay attention to. "Fine, thank you. And how is Mrs. Pierson?"

"I wonder if James knows how good he's got it."

"I think he has some idea."

"I would give five years of my life to trade places with him for one day."

"Professor."

"A well-bodied, able young man of, what did you say he was? Thirty? Thirty-two? A marvelous age. You've been doled out enough in the way of hardships that you aren't a complete knucklehead, but you still have all the advantages of youth. If I had one day, I'd spend the morning playing tennis, the afternoon hiking up a mountain, and the evening with some beautiful woman who couldn't get enough of me. I'd feel—whole."

He wanted so little, really. Just ordinary life back. "That sounds like a good day."

"I had plenty of wonderful days. I like to think I lived my pre-accident life to the fullest. It isn't true, though—you always want more. As my book attests." He gave me one of his self-deprecating smiles. "Memories provide a measure of joy. The life of the mind, of the imagination, is rich indeed. But the life of the senses ... to have just a glimpse ..."

I felt sorry for him. I kept telling myself he was lecherous and repulsive, but really he was lecherous and appealing.

"Just a glimpse?" I asked.

He looked up, smiling, and I felt like I'd grabbed the bait. It seemed a small thing, though. I had done worse.

I lifted up my shirt—I wasn't wearing a bra. His face flushed, eyes wide, and when I started to drop the shirt, he lifted one finger—*Just one more moment.* So I waited, looking at the trees outside the window, watching the shadows in the room flutter as the breeze blew the leaves. Then I pulled the shirt down, and we both, it seemed, exhaled at the same time.

"Thank you," he said.

I shrugged and went to the kitchen to scrub the sink.

Breasts were no big deal to me. After that day, I took to flashing him on a regular basis and always got the same grateful reaction. One morning I wore a short skirt, and he kept looking at me. "Please," he said. So I sat down across from him and opened my legs just enough. He made an inadvertent sighing sound, and we both laughed. The next day I wore the skirt again.

I didn't tell Jimmy about any of this. I went back and forth between the two worlds, the professor's house in Merdale and Jimmy's, and they felt separate—no overlapping Venn diagram circles, no colored-in curved spaces. Here. There.

But these games occupied more and more of our workday. I tried staying in the kitchen and living room as much as I could, rousing the stinky dogs—who usually spent the mornings sleeping in the Piersons' bed—to take extra-long walks, lingering in town whenever I ran the professor's errands. At the same time, I felt pulled to the study. I could feel him in there, waiting for me. He never touched me, never asked to. That was a tacit boundary.

I wondered again why his last assistant had left. When I asked him, he wheeled over to a filing cabinet, unlocked the top drawer, and pulled out the maid costume. Black with a frilly apron and stockings. A cheap Halloween costume meant for sexy adult parties.

"I asked her to wear this."

We both laughed. "I guess I'm easy by comparison, huh?"

"I live for these moments with you."

"Please don't say that."

"I can't help it."

"What I'm doing is wrong, then. We should stop."

"So no chance you'll put this on?" He waggled his eyebrows at me in an attempt at humor.

I held the costume at arm's length, shaking my head. "Dr. Pierson, if I do this, it will be the last thing." But we both knew better.

～

As July wore on, Jimmy's friends visited less. Maybe they were on vacation, maybe the weather was too hot—we didn't have air-conditioning, just ceiling fans. When people did drop by, they didn't stay too late or drink too much or set up tents in the yard. Sometimes they'd even call first, or wait for an invitation.

Jimmy was amused at the changes in his friends. "Maybe you're a witch," he said. "You've cast a spell on me, and now you've ensorcelled my friends, too."

"Fancy word."

"For fancy witches."

"Maybe they just don't like me."

"If there's something they don't like about you," he said, "it's that I don't give them my undivided attention."

"What about the other girls? The ones in between Vivian and me?"

"It wasn't like this."

"I'm flattered."

"Like I said, you cast a spell. We're all helpless in the face of your witchy powers."

One night Rocky, Sylvia, and Amira came over to play Trivial Pursuit. Rocky insisted on calling it Trivial *Pursuits*. Sylvia corrected him and said, "He also says Victoria's *Secrets*. It's secret. *Secret*. A single secret." Rocky raised his eyebrows at us to show he was egging her on.

I have a competitive streak, and Rocky and I battled it out to the end, when I won with a pink Entertainment card. Question: "What film was Marilyn Monroe fired from right before her death?" Answer: *Something's Got to Give*. Easy. Lyman was a Marilyn fan and had schooled me in all the particulars.

Jimmy said he needed help with his truck, though it was the first I'd heard of it, and the men went outside to drink beers and ponder the mysteries of a faulty fuel line. The women smiled knowingly. "Boys," Amira said. "They hate losing." We refilled our drinks and sat outside. Sylvia had a pink hand fan (to go with her purple-pink spiky hair), which she opened with a flourish, fanning herself and occasionally me or Amira. Fireflies and stars and little white Christmas lights that Jimmy had strung in the trees shone and flickered in the humid dark night.

"Did Jamie tell you?" Amira asked me. "I went on a date last weekend." She widened her eyes—*can you believe it?*—as if dating were an antiquated pastime, like stickball or the Lindy hop.

"How was it? Did you like him?"

"First and last time I'll ever go on a blind date. My paralegal set us up. Obviously I'll have to fire her."

Sylvia and I laughed, though it occurred to me that Amira might be serious.

"He kept doing that thing where he'd anticipate what I was going to say, and then try to say it along with me. I had to talk fast to beat him to the end of my own sentence."

"I hate that," Sylvia said.

"Sometimes I'd veer off in a totally irrelevant direction just to throw him off track. The conversation got pretty strange." Amira rose from the rocking chair and stretched, then looked back at us. "He was smart, though. And a generous lover."

"You slept with him?"

"I'm sorry, Thea. Did I shock you?"

"No, it's just—well, yes. Not shocked. Surprised."

She lit a cigarette, tilting her head back to exhale the smoke. "We all have our needs."

"Amen to that," Sylvia said, fanning the smoke away from her.

Amira didn't notice. "The thing is, no one's perfect. You have to decide what compromises you're willing to make. Maybe this one's fabulous in bed, but he lacks social skills."

"Good at intercourse, bad at discourse," Sylvia said, giggling.

"Or you meet a great conversationalist, but whenever he sweats, he smells weirdly metallic."

"That's weirdly specific."

"That guy from Wichita," Amira said.

"Ah," Sylvia said. "He was a good talker."

Amira turned to me. "At some point you have to face the facts. You're not going to get everything you want in one package. Sorry, Thea. I don't mean to sound like, 'you'll understand when you're older.'"

I hadn't taken her tone that way, so I wasn't sure how to respond. Sylvia sang the chorus of "Love the One You're With," drumming on her knee with the folded fan. Amira harmonized nicely. She must've hated being the fifth wheel. If I weren't there, it would've been Rocky and Sylvia,

Jimmy and Amira. She'd sleep in the guest room and get up the next day and make breakfast with Jimmy, and they'd sit on the porch drinking coffee and talking. But she didn't get to do that. I did.

Everyone left by eleven o'clock, and Jimmy and I sat on the porch finishing our beers. We kept the porch lights off so we wouldn't attract bugs. A couple of bats—mosquito eaters, Nick called them—swooped around the trees.

"You'll be glad to know that Amira got laid," I said.

"That's a relief."

"She told you about her date?"

"She might've mentioned something. Was it the overlapping talker?"

I lit a pretend cigarette and blew the smoke at him. "We all have our needs, Jamie."

He laughed. "I'm glad you guys are getting along better."

"I think she's resigned, or it's a détente, or else she's gathering her forces."

"Don't be paranoid. She's coming around."

"She has been nicer to me," I agreed. And it was true. Lately Amira had managed to overcome or at least hide whatever resentment she felt. Sometimes she ceded her hostess duties and deferred to me. *Should we use the sunflower serving dish, or the Mexican one?* Or *Julie asked me what time they should stop by, and I told her I'd check with you.* She even apologized for the solstice party. "Not just the Jell-O shot miscalculation, which was obviously disastrous," she said. "I was rude to you. I hope you'll accept my apology."

I did, of course. It was easy enough to take the high road.

The house behind us felt lit up and warm, like a benevolent living thing. I wanted to be inside it with Jimmy. I wanted never to leave. Over the last two weeks I'd baked enough zucchini bread to fill a quarter of the chest freezer in the laundry room. As I wrapped the loaves in foil and placed them in Ziploc bags, writing the date with a Sharpie, I imagined Jimmy on a winter afternoon, selecting a loaf and setting it on the counter to thaw. He'd notice the date and the xoxox I sometimes added. He'd bring in a few logs from the woodshed, add them to the cast-iron stove, and settle in his chair to read. Later he'd make a cup of tea and cut a slice of the bread, take a bite and lift his eyes from his book and—and what? Smile at me on the couch across the room? Offer me a bite? Or think of me, far away, and try to imagine where I was at that moment and what I was doing? I would wonder about him, too, and in my sentimental moments I'd hope we were thinking of each other at the exact same time.

"I'm happy," I said, turning to him now.

He put out his hand and held mine. We were sitting next to each other on chaise longue deck chairs that we had bought at Kmart, where the clerk corrected our pronunciation. She had taken French last semester, she said, and the correct pronunciation was "*shay longay*." We kept straight faces and nodded at her, then cracked up in the parking lot.

He kissed my hand. Looked at me. "I have fallen for you, Thea. You know that, right?"

I nodded, nervous in that way I get whenever a boy says he loves me. I told my pounding heart to shut up. I told my skittish mind to take a hike. Jimmy said the words, and I said them back. And I didn't want to run. I didn't want to take the first exit, exceed the 30-mile-per-hour ramp speed, drive as fast as I could to somewhere else. I wasn't eyeing the getaway car and calculating how long it would take me to pack. I was right where I wanted to be. I was with Jimmy. I was young. I was in love. Nothing else seemed to matter.

~

And then at the end of July, something else happened.

In the mornings Jimmy and I always took Josie for a walk. We kept her in the house during the day. If Jimmy was home, working in the garden or grading papers on the deck, she hung out with him. On this particular day, Jimmy stayed on campus late, giving the final exam for his summer class. Afterward we met for dinner at a Cajun restaurant (we were attempting to master a Paul Prudhomme recipe for blackened swordfish), then drove home together.

Jimmy never locked the door. People in the country don't. What's the point? If someone wants to get into the house, it's easy enough to toss a rock through a window.

Josie always heard our footsteps on the deck and waited to greet us, crying in an uncanny voice as if she'd been convinced we were lost forever and now, glory be, found again. But that evening, we walked into a quiet house. No insane Josie-welcome. We searched the rooms, thinking she was sick and huddled in a closet or under a bed. She couldn't have gotten out on her own. Except, apparently, she had. We stood on the deck, calling her name. We checked the pond, the barn, the field. No Josie. Just as Jimmy was about to get in the truck and look for her (Bob's terrible word "roadkill" came to mind), a yellow speck appeared on the lane. The speck grew larger. Josie was racing home as fast as she could. I ran to meet her. She leapt into my arms and nuzzled my neck. I carried her to the house. She was panting hard, her eyes wild. Jimmy brought her water and she drank two bowls, then collapsed on my lap. I gently picked out the burrs from her scruffy fur.

Jimmy and I imagined possible scenarios, but none of them made much sense. Our best guess was that Bob came by to check on Hans. He wouldn't bother letting us know he'd been there. He often visited his charges. So maybe he'd come into the house to get a bottle of milk or make a phone call. The screen door didn't always latch shut. Maybe he'd gone to the bathroom, and Josie escaped without him realizing it. Jimmy didn't want Bob to feel bad. We agreed not to bring it up. We both knew that Josie would not, under any circumstances, attempt to run away from home. "Where have you been?" I kept asking her. "Where did you run off to?" Sometimes looking at Josie was like looking at a person in a dog suit. Her deep brown eyes seemed so human, her furry face a mask.

Later that night, on my way back from feeding Hans, I noticed a couple of cigarette butts in the bucket of sand on the deck. I couldn't remember how long they'd been there. Probably since our dinner guests the week before. The next morning, the butts were gone. Jimmy, I supposed, had cleaned up.

PART III

The best way out is always through.

—Robert Frost

CHAPTER 11

SECRET TREASURE

EARLY IN AUGUST, GEORGE came to spend the night. This would be the first time he had slept over at Jimmy's without his mother since the old house burned down. Normally Julie would have looked after him, but she was out of town, conferring with other booksellers about a batch of first editions. Erika was getting together with an old boyfriend "just to talk." She wouldn't give us any more details. "George will be fine," she assured me. "It's time we loosened the apron strings." He would stay over Saturday night, and she'd pick him up on Sunday.

Saturday was my cleaning day. I liked cleaning Jimmy's house. I wore a jog bra and shorts and put on loud music. Jimmy was in town, buying painting supplies. He had it in his mind to paint the barn before fall. So I felt responsible for George. I'd never had a babysitting job before—though this was hardly babysitting, George was twelve—but still. I was the adult now. Ha-ha.

I checked on George periodically. He was in the hammock reading. His hair was like a big fur ball. Kids at school must tease him about it. Of course there were other more obvious things to tease him about. Even now, as he read, he drummed his fingertips against his temples in a private Morse code. He pulled on a hunk of hair to cover his eyes, then let it go, then pulled again. Every now and then he put the book aside and gazed up at the trees. I remembered reading in my backyard, in the Mexican hammock Lyman had strung between two maples: you lay in it crosswise, tucking feet and head into the stretchy woven fabric. Seeing George rocking back and forth between Jimmy's mulberry trees brought back the old longing for home.

Erika told me that George did well at school. She was especially proud of his prowess on the guitar. "He doesn't tic when he's playing," she said. "It's like people who stutter. Sometimes when they sing, they don't stutter at all."

Before Jimmy left for the paint store, we'd had a fight, or no, not a fight, not even really an argument, but *something*. Erika had acted flustered and distracted when she dropped off George. She couldn't wait to be on her way, couldn't manage to look at either of us. When I mentioned her behavior to Jimmy, he just shrugged.

"You don't think there's something going on?" I pressed. We were in the kitchen. George had already taken refuge in the hammock and couldn't hear us.

"I think it's none of my business."

"What's that supposed to mean?"

"I'm just not interested in what Erika might be up to, if she's not yet interested in telling me about it."

I frowned. "So ... you don't even want to have a conversation about the possibilities? You aren't curious?"

Jimmy was sorting through a box of old paintbrushes to see what he needed at the store. He looked up at me. "I'm really not. I don't see the point. It's gossip, completely unsubstantiated. I'd hate it if people were talking about me in that way."

"Are you kidding? Of course they're talking about you. That's, like, people's main source of entertainment—getting into each other's business." I thought of the solstice party and how Jimmy's friends had asked me all those questions. Everyone was friendly, but they were judging me, too, trying to decide if I was worthy. I had no doubt that they compared notes later—that they were still comparing notes.

"Live and let live, I say." He spun a roller on a handle to see if it still worked.

"I'm not a gossip," I protested.

"A person who likes to gossip is ... ?"

"Discussing people's lives doesn't automatically make you a gossip. You could be concerned. You could be interested in some aspect of their psychological makeup, and you could be analyzing that from a larger, benign perspective."

"Ah, like an anthropologist?"

"No. Like a social being."

He dabbed my nose with a paintbrush. "Gossip."

I stood, one hand on my hip, frustrated. "You're patronizing me."

Jimmy's face changed then. A shadow seemed to fall. His voice got quieter. "A lot of shit has happened with these people, okay? I know way too much already. If Erika's with someone she's not supposed to be with, I don't want to know about it. There's only so much I can store up here." He tapped his head with the paintbrush handle. "I'll be back in an hour."

I nodded. He left without kissing me good-bye. I stood at the window, tears in my eyes. I felt chastised and small. I had stepped over some boundary by commenting on one of his friends. His friends, his boundaries. I couldn't casually talk about Erika or anyone else from his world without sounding somehow critical. Was that it? He drove off, the truck's gears shifting aggressively.

Jimmy and I had been together for a couple of months, and yet we hadn't figured out how to argue, or even disagree. We'd moved in together during the first days—first hours—of our relationship, when everything is thrilling and sweet. You always think, when you fall in love, *it's different this time.* You're convinced that those heady feelings are not because it's new, but because this person is different from the others, and so at some level you believe you will always feel this way. When the feelings fade, you believe that something has gone wrong. The person has failed you, or you have failed each other. But we adapt to everything. Good fortune and bad. And according to the professor's research, passionate love was the happiness that human beings burned through the fastest. In the beginning, everything about our beloved is fascinating. We love to watch him brush his teeth, sleep, put on his socks. But then it becomes old news. Maybe he doesn't rinse out the sink. Maybe he snores. Maybe his socks smell, or he picks at his feet in a singularly unbecoming fashion. He hasn't changed. He's doing just what he's always done. But the restless brain, having seen it ten or twenty or a hundred times, grows bored. Oh, this again? Really? Isn't there some new bit of stimulus you can offer to fire up the synapses?

Daily life had elbowed its inevitable way in. We had dishes to do, and laundry to fold, and barns to paint. Brushing up against each other in the kitchen didn't always result in full-on sex. Casual conversation wasn't always a sublime merging of minds. The electrical impulses had begun to weaken just a tiny bit. If we were going to stay together for any length of time, we had to leave this delicious early phase behind and mellow into the next one. I couldn't fathom the next one. I'd never had any interest in the next one.

"You just love that squirt of dopamine," Emily used to say, making a syringe motion at my head.

"It's my favorite whaddyacallit."

"Neurotransmitter."

"That's the one."

And my agreement with Jimmy loomed in the background. Either of us could decide to back out, no questions asked. So I was more sensitive than usual about any comment tinged with criticism. I worried that his perception of me as, for instance, a gossip, was the first step toward "I think this was a mistake."

Also ... where were we now? Were we still having a summer fling? When did a fling become something more? I recalled the graphs from my astronomy class. Maybe there was a way to plot the points of a love affair to predict the likelihood of a serious relationship. Eddie, whose idea of fun included graph-plotting, came incongruously to mind.

Jimmy and I hadn't discussed our plans. We could go along for months, and he would never bring it up. Our situation would be another of his path-of-least-resistance choices, life coming to him on waves, and him just riding them. Lately, though, I'd allowed my thoughts to venture beyond Labor Day. I skipped over the part about having to see Eddie. To assuage my guilt and keep him from worrying, I'd sent a couple of post-cards as follow-ups to that first one. My messages remained vague—and brief. *All okay here. Saving some money. Figuring out the next step. Hope you're well.* Like that.

I imagined October. And then, Thanksgiving. I picked out the best corner in the living room for a Christmas tree. I flipped through a course catalog from Merdale College that Jimmy had on his desk. The Clash's "Should I Stay or Should I Go" came to mind, and not for the first time.

I vacuumed up the cobwebs and dust balls, every so often looking out the window to be sure George was still there, swinging back and forth in the hammock, tapping his head, like a child absentmindedly sucking his thumb. He was reading the fantasy novel I'd brought him from the bookstore. I was pleased I'd introduced him to a new author.

I thought of my mother, who loved to clean. Well, she loved to clean *sometimes*. These episodes began innocently enough, but I learned to detect the signs of a growing obsession. She'd sort through clothes in a closet or tidy up her dresser drawers, but by the end of the week, the mattresses had all been flipped and dust ruffles laundered and ironed. The chrome in the kitchen gleamed sinisterly. She soaked combs and hairbrushes in ammonia, scrubbed the bathroom grout with old tooth-brushes, and attacked the windows with vinegar and balled-up news-paper. I kept my distance, because if I didn't, I'd find myself on hands and knees working at ancient stains in the carpet with baking soda, or alphabetizing my father's record albums.

As the week wore on, she became more focused, more methodical, less communicative. Once in a while I'd find her standing in the middle of a room, a rag or bottle of tung oil in her hand, eyes fixed on nothing, as if she were listening to complicated instructions from a faint voice.

"Watch out," my father would say. "It's starting."

The next *project*. A wall-sized abstract in acrylics or a mixed-media collage or a shadow box assemblage. She did a series of self-portraits that took her the better part of my elementary school years. It doesn't seem all that original to me now, but at the time I was enthralled. She'd wanted to capture aspects of her identity, the roles she had played in her life, and used different media to express each. Daughter. Dancer. Wife. Painter. Teacher. Taxpayer. I remembered the Mother portrait the best: a kind of cubist collage, fractured, with layered, overlapping bits of colored tis-sue and newsprint and other scraps of paper and fabric. "Why does she look like that?" I asked. "She's all broken up, like glass." I was probably George's age. My mother smiled at me. "I just make what I see," she said. I was too literal-minded—I couldn't imagine how she looked at herself and saw *that*. And what did her splintered sense of herself have to do with me? Did she feel that being my mother broke her into fragments? Of course, that's exactly what she felt.

She was my age when I was born. I couldn't imagine having a baby right now. A cruel thought came into my head. What if he turned out like George?

I finished vacuuming, even removing cushions and sucking up the popcorn kernels and lint and other couch detritus. When I looked up, George was standing there, watching me. I jerked, as if zapped with electricity.

"George, you startled me!"

"Sorry." He yanked on a hunk of hair.

"Can I get you something?" Sweat streamed down my chest and back. I adjusted the jog bra and wished I had a shirt to cover myself.

"I'm thinking I'll just go home now. Maybe you could drive me?"

"George. Your mom doesn't want you staying by yourself. It's just for tonight. She'll be back tomorrow." He knew all this, but I didn't know what else to say.

"I'm old enough to stay by myself. She's overprotective. I'll be fine."

I couldn't argue with him there. "How about some lunch?" I went into the kitchen, hoping he'd follow. "Peanut butter and jelly? Or egg salad? I have some hard-boiled eggs." I examined the contents of the refrigerator while George stood behind me, slouching and fidgety. I remembered that Erika said he hated mayonnaise. "Jimmy grilled some extra chicken last night. I think it tastes better cold."

"It might be better"—and here he was overcome with a fit, head jerking and eyes closed—"if I went home now."

"Why do you want to go home?"

"I'm not trying to be rude. I'm sorry." I could see him struggling not to cry, this big boy with his furry hair and trembling lower lip.

I tried to placate him. "Let's make some lunch, and when Jimmy gets home, we can figure out something fun to do today."

He sat at the table, covering his face with his hands. "She knows I hate being by myself out here. Why did she have to go? She's so selfish."

I was getting out the leftovers, a plate, silverware. "But you're not by yourself. I'm here. Jimmy will be back."

"I mean overnight. Sleeping over without—Erika."

"You used to, right? When you were little? Didn't you stay with Jimmy sometimes?"

"That was before."

I wiped my hands on a towel. Be careful, I thought. I put the chicken on the plate, cut up a peach, peeled some carrots and sliced them into sticks, poured him a glass of milk. I endeavored to follow Erika's instructions: no mayo, nothing green, nothing touching each other.

I brought him his meal and sat down. "Before what?"

"That was before. I haven't spent the night out here in a long time." He picked up a slice of peach and examined it. "Don't say anything to Jimmy. About me crying."

"You didn't cry, George." I patted his hand. He didn't shrink from me. He took a nibble of the fruit, then looked up.

"Yes," he said. "I did."

～

I had my shower and got dressed, and after that I couldn't find George. He wasn't in the guest room or in the hammock, and when I called his name, he didn't answer. I walked up to the barn to check on Hans—as careful as I was not to tame him, he associated me with his food, and he perked up whenever I came near, his big ears twitching. I wanted to keep him as a pet, though everything about that idea was stupid.

Bob would release Hans in September, maybe sooner. Next month! I needed to figure something out. The professor came unbidden to mind, and I flushed with guilt. I would have to quit that job before anything else happened. I really, really would.

I stroked the deer's nose and told him it wasn't dinnertime yet.

"You aren't supposed to pet him," a voice said. George was up in the loft, looking down at me.

"George! Stop sneaking up on me!"

He smiled. "I wasn't sneaking up on you. I was already here." His earlier mood seemed to have lifted. He spoke like a normal kid.

"What are you doing up there, anyway?"

"It's my spot. No one ever comes up here."

That was true. Jimmy used the barn mostly for Bob's animals, and to store his mower and tools. Without livestock, a hayloft wasn't of much use.

"So what's up there?"

George studied me, torn about how to respond. Then he said, "It's a secret."

I hadn't expected that. "I'm good at keeping secrets."

"Like what? What's a secret you've kept?"

I laughed. Suddenly there were so many. "If I tell you, then I won't have done a good job of keeping it, will I?"

He tapped out a quick rhythm on his forehead. "I have secrets, too."

"Everyone does."

"Things I've never told anybody. Not even my mother."

"That's okay. There are lots of things I've never told my mother."

"But you're older. You're supposed to not tell your mother things."

"You're twelve. I definitely had secrets from my mother by the time I was twelve."

"Tell me one."

"Then you'll have to tell me yours."

He looked behind him, as if checking with someone. "I might." He sounded scared and excited, too. "You seem like a nice person."

"Can I come up there? It hurts my neck to keep looking up like this."

"After you tell."

I sighed. "Okay." I sat on the stool I used when I was feeding Hans. He had given up on having his bottle but was watching me just in case, his tail flicking back and forth. The interior of the barn was dim, but just outside the door was all that bright heat, like something solid. Motes and dust hung in the few rays of light that reached into the barn interior. I scanned my memories for a pre-twelve-year-old story.

"When I was ten, I stayed the summer with Wendy and her parents."

"I like Wendy."

"Me too. That summer, my parents were in Greece. They were always somewhere. Sometimes I went with them, but a lot of times I stayed with relatives or friends while they were away."

"Didn't you miss them?"

I thought for a moment about how it felt to be ten years old and a guest at Wendy's parents' house. My pseudo-grandparents. I closed my eyes and remembered walking into the guest room where I would stay for six long weeks. The curtains were drawn so that all I could see was the twin bed and the dresser and a small mirror over the dresser. A painting of a farmhouse in winter hung on one wall. The sky in the painting was gray and the snow was piled high against the door, so that I worried about the people inside the house and whether they could get out. Maybe they would have to wait for spring, for the snow to melt. Maybe they would crawl out the second-floor windows and drop to the ground. I unpacked my suitcase and opened the curtains. An endless summer lay before me.

"I was homesick at first," I said. George's hair flopped forward and created a shadow over his face, so I couldn't see his eyes. I wondered what he had up there. Dirty magazines? Old shell casings from Jimmy's .22? Arrowheads, cigarettes, shoplifted candy, money from his mother's wallet? "Have you ever been homesick? It's like a heavy weight just sitting on top of you. And my parents were so far away, I couldn't even talk to them on the phone. I didn't know my grandfather—Wendy's father—or his wife, or Wendy herself, or her little brother, Henry. Henry was a couple of years older than I was. About your age." I tried to explain how Henry was my uncle, but George had a difficult time grasping that concept.

Hans shifted in his hay. Outside grasshoppers sprung up and down in the grass like mechanical toys. A red-tailed hawk dove toward some small moving thing in the field. George lay on his belly with his chin in his hands. He had stopped tapping. I shouldn't be telling him this, I thought. But I had gone too far, and I couldn't quickly think up a lie.

"One day, Henry and I played Truth or Dare. I forget what he asked me, but I took the dare. And—I took off my clothes. Outside. In the backyard." George covered his face with his hands, laughing. "No one else was around," I clarified.

"You were naked? Outside?"

I smiled. "I had to run from the back door, to the edge of the yard, and back again. Buck naked. That was the dare."

He laughed harder.

"Why is that so funny?"

"It just is."

"Can I come up now?"

He sat up, looked behind him again. "You aren't going to be mad, are you?"

"I don't think so."

He nodded. Pointed to the ladder.

I was still thinking about Henry as I climbed up to the loft. And the professor, of course. I hadn't seen the seed of my exhibitionism in that young self. I felt embarrassed, uncovering this obvious truth, how willing I was to reveal myself to boys and yet how much I kept hidden. How silly I'd been, too, to think that the professor could help me. When I first went to work for him, I'd imagined therapist-like scenarios, me lying on a couch while he listened and took notes and did whatever therapists were supposed to do—guide me toward a deeper understanding! Help me find direction! As if me lying on a couch in close proximity to the professor would ever result in anything except more trouble.

George had a duffel bag next to him. I wondered if he was running away, except for the fact that the duffel was pink, and not, to my knowledge, his. His small blue Samsonite suitcase was in the guest room.

"Whose is that?"

"I keep it up here," he said. "See that hole over there?" There was a crevice in between the floor and the eaves of the barn. "I keep it in there. You can't even see it. It tucks right into that space." He was nervous, his breath coming quickly. "You can't tell anyone. You have to promise."

"George. Are you thinking about running away?"

"It's not mine."

"Then whose is it? If it belongs to someone else, we need to return it. They're probably looking for it."

He unzipped the bag. He pulled out a neat stack of folded clothes, a toiletries case, socks, underwear. A leather journal, whose pages— he flipped through them to demonstrate—were blank. A pair of red Converse sneakers, with designs drawn in silver paint. He set the shoes between us so I could see them more closely. We were both sweating in the cloying air. I touched the shoes, the rough texture of the paint on the canvas. The white laces looked new. "George." I was whispering. I didn't mean to, but I couldn't make the words come out in a normal voice. "Who does this stuff belong to?" I was afraid now. I waited for him to finish tapping out another comforting message to himself on his forehead. Then he looked up at me, his face shining and flushed with heat and the adventure of sharing this secret treasure.

"She left it here," he said. "That night. She put it on the porch and I took it. I thought maybe I could keep her from going. I didn't want her to leave. It sounds dumb, I know. But I was only ten. She was one of my favorite people."

"Who?" I asked. But I already knew what he was going to say.

"Vivian."

For a moment we just stared at each other. I was trying to recall what Jimmy had told me about the night Vivian left, the night the house burned down. He'd had people over, as a "buffer," he'd said. George was here. What else?

But then we heard the truck driving up the lane. I helped George put away Vivian's things. He had a particular order that could not be violated.

"Remember, you promised not to tell anyone. Don't tell Jimmy, he'll be mad at me. But, Thea," he pleaded—he hadn't ever spoken my name before—"especially don't tell Amira."

"Why not Amira?"

He stuffed the bag back in its hiding place, and we made our way down the ladder.

"Just say we were checking on Hans. I'll tell you later."

I agreed. There wasn't time to say much else. I figured there had to be some reasonable explanation. And I certainly wasn't in any hurry to bring up Vivian with Jimmy again.

Still, Vivian's bag, hidden in the barn all this time?

Jimmy honked his horn twice, his customary greeting. George and I stepped out of the barn and into the harsh light. The day was humid, and a heavy, fleshy, roast-beef smell hung in the air. I helped Jimmy unload the truck. He seemed to have forgotten our earlier conversation, the small tensions that had arisen. After the paint store he'd picked up some groceries and run into Wendy and Bob. They'd invited the three of us for dinner. I was glad. I wanted to see Wendy and her cats and sit on her swing surrounded by all her gnomes and stones and shells and wind chimes. Everything felt easy there. Safe. I thought of her spare room, the mobile with the birds hanging over the twin bed. In spite of my feelings for Jimmy, at that moment I wondered why I hadn't just driven to New York. I could've enjoyed our night together, returned to Wendy's, picked up Emily's car from the mechanic, and taken off. Here it was, August already. What had happened to the summer?

But, I reminded myself, if I'd gone to Eddie's I'd be living with him right now, and if I lived with him I might actually marry him, and if I married him I'd end up divorcing him, and if I divorced him I'd lose Emily forever.

Jimmy was talking about a song he heard on the radio on the way home. I nodded, and smiled, and wondered what would happen between us now.

"I stopped at the post office," he said, handing me an envelope.

My mother had finally gotten around to forwarding Emily's letter. We carried the groceries into the house. George lay in the hammock, watching us. I waved at him. He lifted his hand, then placed one finger on his lips. I nodded.

I helped Jimmy put away the groceries then opened the letter. Emily had written to me during her first week on the island. She told me about teaching English to the children of Ngoof and assisting with the women's health clinic. She told me about Pingelap, where 10 percent of the inhabitants were color-blind. She described her fellow volunteers, who worked on other islands or in Colonia, the capital. She didn't mention Eddie. I'd been granted a reprieve. I tucked the letter into a drawer. I'd write her back as soon as I knew what to say.

~

George and I didn't have a chance to talk that evening. The three of us went into town for dinner at Wendy and Bob's, and then we all walked to the city park to listen to an oldies band. Wendy brought beach blankets for us to sit on. Little kids danced near the stage, their faces painted with flowers and rainbows. The band was good. I saw people I knew from the bookstore, from the coffee shop, from Kinko's, from the library. "Miss Popular," Bob teased. Jimmy smiled, too, and put his arm around me. Wendy danced with the children, her gauzy-sleeved arms waving like streamers.

We were up late, and George fell asleep in the car on the way home. Jimmy woke him up long enough to shepherd him to the guest room. I got Hans's bottle ready. I was stupidly nervous about going to the barn in the dark. The duffel in the loft felt like somebody lying in wait. I lit the Coleman lantern—the barn had no electricity—and raised it high as I walked. I couldn't stop thinking about George's fastidious removal of Vivian's clothing from the bag. The neatly folded T-shirts, the pair of black jeans with a rose embroidered on one back pocket, the pink lace bra, the red shoes. I pictured Jimmy looking through Vivian's stuff, shaking his head. *Oh yeah, I remember those jeans, I remember when she embroidered that flower. . . .*

I sat in the pen with Hans, holding the bottle at arm's length. The lantern created the usual jumpy shadows, and I focused on the deer's noisy sucking and slurping. I didn't look up at the loft. No one was up there. I had watched too many scary movies. But all the times I'd sat there with Hans, that duffel bag was tucked away above me, waiting, it seemed now, to be revealed.

Especially don't tell Amira. An image of Amira rose before me, the look she gave me when she handed me the spiked Jell-O, how she sat with me smoking cigarettes and chatting as if we were pals. I could almost taste the nicotine, almost smell the smoke as she exhaled it. What did Amira have to do with all this? What did George know, or imagine he knew, about her? Hans finished up the last of the milk. I shut the pen behind me and walked back to the house. I had to force myself not to break into a run.

I wondered when I'd have the opportunity to see George alone again. Maybe I could offer to take him out for ice cream or a burger. I kept thinking about the look of concentration on his face as he removed Vivian's clothes from the bag. He had done it many times. He had preserved the order of the items, the exact way she had packed them. His movements were ritualized, as if he were performing a sacrament. He'd giggled at my Truth or Dare story, but he was undaunted by the private nature of Vivian's belongings, her underwear, her toiletries. He had visited Vivian's personal effects for two years. Two years was a lifetime for a twelve-year-old. Her panties and bra had long since lost their power to titillate or embarrass him. I couldn't imagine what the rest of the story could possibly be. What Vivian would have written in that journal, had she taken it with her.

~

On Sunday, the weather was hot and windy, the kind of prairie wind that has no cooling effect—just blows dust around and makes everyone crazy. Erika arrived to pick up George as scheduled. She avoided looking at us and declined Jimmy's offer of brunch. She said she needed to get home, but I think she was afraid that if she stuck around, she'd let something slip about her weekend. After she and George left, the house felt empty. The day stretched dully ahead. I felt at a loss and sensed that Jimmy did, too, and that was why he'd invited Erika to stay.

We changed the guest room sheets, made the bed, cleaned up the breakfast dishes. Then Jimmy retired to the couch to read. I felt penned in. I was tempted to climb up the ladder to the hayloft and take another look at that bag. I even considered bringing it into the house to show Jimmy. But I remembered George imploring me. I could wait a day or two.

The wind rattled the windows and made me restless and irritable. The next morning I'd have to go to the professor's and deal with his nonsense, which had grown tiresome. Then to the bookstore, where I was busier than usual since Julie was still away. The sorority girls had arrived in town to prepare for rush, and once or twice a day they paraded through Campus Corner. They seemed intent on fulfilling every stereotype with their collective tanning-booth glow and shiny pink lip gloss and manic voices. I felt contempt, yes, but maybe envy, too. What would it be like to be so certain of your place in the world? To be that hysterically happy? Or at least, to appear that way.

That week I'd watched a gaggle of girls standing on the sidewalk outside the store. They were trying to make a decision, all talking at once and waving their arms around. One girl at the edge of the group took a few tentative steps backward, and then a few more. She backed into the bookstore's swinging doors and crossed the threshold before she turned around. What expertise! I started to ask if I could help her find something, but she was a seasoned browser and wanted to be left alone. She found the Danielle Steel section, scanned some spines, and selected a book. Outside her sisters looked up and down the street, but my customer was oblivious. I wanted to stash her under the counter or in the storage room, but alas, one of the girls spied her through the plate glass window and barged inside. "*Jessica!*" she hollered. "What are you *doing*? C'mon, we've gotta get the *skirts* for the *skit!*" Jessica looked up dazed, her freckled face and dark hair beautiful in the late afternoon light, though she was not particularly beautiful.

"Geez, Jess," the girl said, "you're such a complete *flake*. I hope you're going to be able to *do* this."

"Thanks for coming in," I said. The sorority sister gave me a once-over, taking in my T-shirt, jeans, short messy hair. I wasn't anybody who mattered. She took the Danielle Steel and tossed it onto a display table, then yanked Jessica by the wrist as if she were a recalcitrant child. The book's title was embossed in silver. *Summer's End*. Ha-ha. "Come back soon," I added. But the doors had already swung shut.

I wondered what Jessica was doing on this desolate hot Sunday. Maybe rehearsing for the skit, or maybe she'd orchestrated another disappearing act. Outside the grass was patchy, the sky a milky washed-out blue, the leaves on the trees a faded and dusty green.

"Let's go somewhere," I said to Jimmy. He ignored me. He was reading a textbook and taking notes for a Civil War class he would teach in the fall. Interrupting him was selfish. But I didn't feel like reading or listening to music. I missed the ocean. In a mood like this, you could always go to the shore and stick your toes in the water. You could look for shells and watch the surfers in wet suits mounting their boards over and over, chasing the rush. You could work up an appetite just breathing the salty air then walk barefoot to a beach joint and order beer and fries.

"Let's drive into town. Let's go to a movie." *Risky Business* had just opened, and I wanted to see it. I imitated a wheedling child. "We never go *anywhere*. We never do *anything*." I crawled up his legs and stuck my head under his book. I lifted his shirt and kissed him. He was ticklish and grabbed my shoulders to push me off. We got into a wrestling match, his book and notes falling to the floor, the cushions slipping off the couch. "Buttered popcorn! Air-conditioning!" I yelled. He growled at me in his playful-boyfriend voice, calling me a minx, a wench, a trollop. We were both laughing, breathless. Josie barked and ran in circles around us. Jimmy had me pinned, but I was making headway. Then the phone rang, and he called time-out. I got up and lay on the couch. I hoped no one was planning to come for a visit, then I hoped someone was. It'd be fun to see Lori and Gigi or even Rocky and Sylvia. Irish folk music jigged along on the stereo, one of the Sunday afternoon public radio shows that Jimmy always played. Later he'd listen to *Prairie Home Companion*.

"Thea?" he called. "It's for you." There was something in his voice. I sat up. My first thought was, Something's happened to my parents. They've crashed that camper they bought. They were terrible drivers. Maybe they'd killed somebody. Or Emily had contracted malaria. She needed me to come take care of her on her island. I'd have to dig through the boxes I'd stored in Wendy's garage to find my passport. I hoped it hadn't expired. How long did it take to get a new passport? These thoughts fired through my brain one after the other as I hurried to Jimmy.

He stood in the doorway, holding the phone toward me, his face closed.

"It's your fiancé."

UNFINISHED BUSINESS

MY MOTHER CONSTRUCTED ASSEMBLAGES that were like little windows into a secret world. She filled shadow boxes with objects she collected or scavenged, arranging and rearranging them until the effect suited her. The boxes were a puzzle, it seemed, and she was trying to make the different pieces fit together, as if there were a single correct composition but she wouldn't know what it was until she found it. Sometimes she worked on a box for weeks, hunting for missing items at flea markets and garage sales. She'd take the box apart and put it back together again, over and over. I used to examine these boxes for hours, identifying bits of fabric or wallpaper from the samples she stored in the attic, or items she had taken from my room: a chair from my dollhouse, the hospital ID bracelet I'd saved from when I had my tonsils out, a black velvet hair ribbon. I never minded when she filched these trinkets. Discovering them in their new homes fascinated me.

She gave the boxes mysterious titles. *Le Temps Vole, World Without End, Monsoon Woman.* I can still recall some of the odd juxtapositions, the bits and pieces she put together. Chess pieces, an insurance ad clipped from *Life* magazine, an earring, an obituary torn from the newspaper, a key, a burned-out Christmas lightbulb. Some of the boxes were disturbing, but others were like miniature fairylands, contained and safe and wondrous. I wanted to live inside them, I wanted to be an object my mother had searched for and put in her pocket, I wanted to take refuge behind the (I imagined) soundproof glass in my own sealed-off world.

I wanted to be in one of those boxes now. I'd be the girl from my dollhouse family (mommy, daddy, sister, brother, genderless baby), tiny patent-leathered feet, striped skirt and blond hair, like Jane from the Dick and Jane books. The back of the box would be covered with scraps of paper: the phone number for Jimmy's mechanic, highway diner receipts, the Sooty Tern stamp from Emily's envelope, a peeled-off label from a beer bottle, a strip of map from my road atlas, a corner of a page from the professor's manuscript. And me, suspended with invisible wire, upside down and limbs akimbo.

I wanted to lie, or to laugh and say, Fiancé? Must be a wrong number. If only we'd gone to the movies! As if that would have prevented Eddie from ever calling. I thought of Wendy and wished she were there to help me. I don't know why I thought of her, it made no sense, but Jimmy holding the phone out to me and Eddie waiting on the other end didn't make sense either. How did he get this number? Phoebe? Wendy? *It's all a big misunderstanding.* If only I could wind back the tape of time, travel down the Möbius strip that led from this moment back to that other moment, the day when Jimmy and I first met and we stood together in this very kitchen, and our hands accidentally touched, and we felt the things we felt. I wanted to say, Jimmy. This isn't what it seems.

But isn't that what the wife says, when her husband comes home from work early and finds her in bed with his best friend? *This isn't what it looks like.* Oh really? What is it, then? I couldn't speak. I made myself walk across the room. It felt as if the hot wind outside were blowing inside me. *Il n'y a rien à faire*, I thought, my French ridiculously coming back to me. There is nothing to do. Except. Step. Across. The. Floor.

I arrived in no time at all, of course. Jimmy looked both hurt and dismissive, the shadows that appeared under his eyes nearly purple now. Eddie had entered the picture, and I couldn't explain him. Jimmy liked to say, "Easy come, easy go." He probably wanted to say that to me now. And then an image flew into my head, me wearing the maid costume and bending over to dust a shelf for the professor's pleasure.

Shame, shame, shame. Shame on you, Dorothea Knox.

Jimmy let the phone slip into my hand and turned away. He didn't even look at me. Because I said nothing, because I didn't refute the claim of the man on the phone, Jimmy now believed that the fiancé was real. I was a girl who'd left her fiancé in the lurch, a girl who'd been using Jimmy and his house and his friends to skip town, hide out, lie low. I thought of Vivian, how she'd come to Jimmy's to escape her dead-end job and crappy apartment. And here I was.

I could imagine the things Amira would say about me, after I left. It seemed clear to me that I would have to leave. Eddie on one side, having found out about Jimmy. Jimmy on the other side, having found out about Eddie. And me, hearing the word "fiancé" and acting caught rather than bewildered, like any reasonable, innocent person.

I held the receiver in my hand like a piece of rotten fruit. Jimmy took his keys from the bowl. He didn't look at me, and I didn't say anything. Nothing. Not *wait*. Not *please*. He left the house, got into his truck, and drove down the lane, dust blowing up behind him like smoke. A cold trickle of sweat rolled down my back. Eddie's voice, trapped in the phone, called out to me. "Thea? Thea? Are you there?" I felt sorry for Eddie then, and sorry for Jimmy, and sorry for me.

I wanted to cry, watching Jimmy drive away, but I neatly folded and put away my emotion, stacked it there with the rest. I cleared my throat and said hello into the phone as loudly as I could manage—still barely audible.

"Thea, is that you?"

And I remembered Eddie then. Those phone calls when we sometimes talked for an hour or two. How he was often distracted and lost in his own head. How he loved explaining things to me, and I loved listening. That day in Manchester buying snow tires, like an old couple, his arm around me. The thrill of our nightly assignations. That had been exciting, the sneaking around. I hated to admit how much I liked that part.

"How are you, Eddie?" Dumb. I didn't blame him for the derisive laughter.

"I'm just swell. Kind of confused, though. Could you tell me where, exactly, you are?"

It sounded absurd, now that I had to put it into words. "I'm in ... Kansas. Didn't you get my postcards?"

"Didn't I get your postcards?" He laughed again. I didn't like this new Eddie that I had created, Dr. Frankenstein–style. "Yeah, I got your cards. They were, what's the word? *Pithy*. Succinct. Not a lot of information. No address where I could write you back, for instance. No phone number. I wasn't sure you even had a phone. But here you are, on the other end of a real live phone line. Stupendous."

"I'm so sorry. Things have been kind of . . . in flux."

"Your parents have dropped off the face of the earth. I wrote to Emmie, and she wrote back and said she had no idea what you were up to. It's easier to contact my sister in fricking Micronesia than to track *you* down."

She probably said some other stuff, too. Probably Emily was furious at me. *There she goes again*, she'd think, while she toiled in the jungle among her adoring students. I hadn't written to her yet. Not even a postcard.

"Change of plans," I mumbled.

"Yeah, I got that. That part was clear. Let's see. Here's the impression I was under. I was assuming that you were driving Emily's car here, and then you and I would spend the summer together and you'd get a job and we'd, you know, see how things went. And then in the fall you'd apply to NYU or wherever."

"To do what?"

"Whatever you want. That's not the point."

I remembered vaguely a conversation we'd had about NYU, back in February or March. I had liked that plan because I could imagine walking around the Village in between classes, drinking espresso and sitting on park benches in Washington Square. But I hadn't ever *committed* to that plan. Had I?

"Thea." He was pleading. The last day of Christmas vacation, we stood in his parents' guest room and held each other. He cupped the back of my head with his hand in the most tender gesture. The palm of his hand, holding the back of my head, gently holding me to him. The word "cleaving" had come to mind.

Shit.

"I'm sorry," I said again. "But, Eddie, you freaked me out. You—you *proposed* to me. That came out of nowhere. I'm not ready to even think about being proposed to. I just graduated from college. You and I—we had a few nights together, we talked on the phone, but in no way did I consider us—"

"I was a little unhinged that night. I went too far. I tried calling you back, but the phone was off the hook."

"I unplugged it."

"I figured."

"But you were serious, though. Right? Unhinged and serious?"

He was quiet for a moment. "Unhinged and serious. I thought we had something, Thea. For me it was more than just 'we spent a few nights together, we talked on the phone.' I felt like we really connected."

He was right. We had connected. But. Here's the sad part. Our connection just didn't mean as much to me as it meant to him. He was too serious, too good, too nice, too . . . Eddie.

"Anyway, when you left that rambling message on my machine, I knew I'd gone too far. Then I got your card and figured, well, she'll call me when she's ready. But you didn't call. You just never did." His voice grew softer now. "Sometimes I fantasized that you'd be waiting in the driveway when I got home from work. Leaning on the Buick, you know, just—hey! Here I am! And then a second card came, and a third. It was pretty clear you weren't going to show up. At least I knew you were alive, so thanks for that."

"Eddie."

"So the guy who answered the phone? He's, what, the *new* boyfriend now?"

I squirmed. I looked out the window at the windblown grass and trees. No sign of that boyfriend now. I felt sick.

"How did you get this number?" I asked.

"One of your new friends contacted me."

"Someone called you?"

"Never mind. I really can't talk about this anymore right now. I have to go do rounds. I'll talk to you—whenever, I guess." And he hung up.

For a few minutes I just stood there. I looked out the window as if Jimmy were due home any minute, as if he would drive up and honk twice, same as always. He didn't come. I paced the living room and kitchen. Once I told him the whole story, Jimmy might or might not forgive me. Emily, protective of her family, would not. I was sorry, but I couldn't go back and change anything now. I had to figure out the next step. If I had to leave now, where would I go? Really. Where?

Well, Wendy's. Wendy would take me in.

And then: Who had betrayed me like this?

I hoped Jimmy had just gone for a drive to clear his head. He'd be back soon, and I could straighten out this mess. I rehearsed what I would say. I did a load of laundry, and kept checking the phone's dial tone, then worried that in the second it had taken me to pick up the receiver Jimmy had called and heard a busy signal and assumed I was still talking to Eddie. Wandering through the rooms I saw all the stuff I had, in my presumption, spread around the house, as if I really lived there, as if I had the right to call this place home. I carried the laundry basket from room to room and gathered my things. Just in case, I kept telling myself. Just in case he wants me out. He had acted decisively with Vivian. He hadn't wavered. If I couldn't convince him of the true nature of my relationship with Eddie (and what was that, exactly?) or if my behavior caused him to question my basic character (and why wouldn't it?), he might not give me a second chance. *A lot of shit has happened with these people . . .*

Upstairs I took out my suitcase. It was empty, except for the outside pocket. I unzipped it. I found my ponytail in the Ziploc bag, and the list I had made that night in Wendy's house: *Eddie Gallagher. Pros and Cons. White Plains. Engaged.* It'd be easy enough to dial up Information and get his phone number.

Amira. Who else?

I remembered the night of the solstice party, how Amira hadn't walked the labyrinth with the rest of us. She skipped out so she could snoop in our—in Jimmy's—bedroom and rummage through my stuff, looking for something she could use against me. Or maybe she'd done it the day she kidnapped my dog. I felt sure now that Amira had lured Josie from the house, driven her who knows how many miles away, and dumped her. She couldn't kill my dog outright, even she had limits, but the odds that Josie would get hit by a car, or spend the night at the mercy of wildcats and coyotes, would've been good enough for her. Amira wanted to mess with me. She wanted me gone. Acting nice was just part of the ruse.

The house was so quiet. Only the hollow sound of the wind.

I called Rocky's to see if Jimmy was there. Sylvia answered. I acted as if Jimmy and I had miscommunicated about the evening's plans and I was trying to track him down. The pretense made no sense, but Sylvia was unfazed. She hadn't heard from Jimmy. "Rocky's at the ER," she said. "This old dude's chain saw kicked back and split his forehead open. Rocky's stitching him up. You'd be surprised how often people do that." She chuckled.

No answer at Erika's. I tried Wendy. Bob was on his way out the door, and Wendy was working at the greenhouse. He sounded too stoned to be of much use, but he didn't think he'd seen Jimmy that day. I even tried Gigi and Lori's. After I called everyone I could think of, I regretted it. I was spreading gossip fodder everywhere, like fertilizer.

I didn't call Amira. I wouldn't be able to stand hearing her voice. And if Jimmy was with her, I wouldn't be able to stand that, either.

I fed Hans. I was too restless to stay put. I scribbled a note for Jimmy. *I'm out looking for you.* I hoped Wendy was home by now. But Wendy's and Bob's cars were both gone. I knocked on the door anyway. I stood on the front porch and looked in the windows. The cats, who'd been sleeping on the welcome mat, roused themselves long enough to rub against my legs. I thought about crawling in through a window and finding my way to the guest room and climbing into bed, under the bird mobile. What a long time ago that was. I steeled myself and drove by Amira's. I'd only been there once, to drop off a pie plate she'd left at the house. No sign of Jimmy's truck. Where are you? I thought. Don't run away from me. Come back so we can talk. Nothing is as it seems.

I understood the benefits of the group. *Membership has its privileges.* I wanted to go to the wise, indulgent Julie, but she was out of town. Last possibility: Erika. She hadn't answered the phone, but maybe she was home by now.

Erika's house was a bungalow like Wendy's, but without the colorful accents. The porch swing was painted white, and the house itself was a staid taupe with white trim. I rang the doorbell. A wasp's nest clung to the corner of the porch ceiling. I stared at the little papery holes, waiting for a wasp to emerge. I tried to remember the difference between wasps and hornets, but it was like crocodiles and alligators, or porpoises and dolphins—I knew the differences were important, I just could never recall what they were. Dusk had fallen, and the wind had begun to die down. Erika's living room lights were on. I rang the doorbell again.

The door opened. "Thea," Erika said, reluctantly, as if I were the last person she wanted to see.

"I'm sorry to just drop by like this—I'm just—I don't know where else to go." Normally I would've apologized for the dramatics, but Erika was too flustered by my appearance to notice. She turned and gesticulated to someone behind her.

My first thought was that Vivian was inside. I'd walk in and see Jimmy and Vivian, arms around each other, reunited at last.

"If this is a bad time—"

"No, it's okay." Again she turned. Then she nodded and opened the door wider. "Come in. But, Thea—don't flip out, okay?"

Vivian and Jimmy weren't in Erika's living room. Nick was. "Hi, Thea," he said. He couldn't look at me. He ran a hand through his silvery hair. The stubs of his fingers didn't look weird on Nick. The stumps were almost—cute.

"Hey," I said, uncertainly. Erika fled to the kitchen and took glasses from the cabinet, calling out to me about tonic and lime. "Just vodka," I answered. "No ice."

Nick jammed fists into pockets and kept his eyes on the plush blue carpeting. The carpet was comforting in its absolute averageness. The whole house was like that—furnished with Ethan Allen sofas and end tables, all very tasteful and adult. Erika had grown up in that house and moved back in with her parents when she got pregnant during her senior year of college. (According to Lori, George's father was a football player. He and Erika had a fling, nothing serious. He'd never been a part of George's life. It's possible he didn't even know George existed.) When Erika's dad got transferred to St. Louis, her parents moved. I imagined that everything looked the same as the day they left, the muted striped gold wallpaper in the dining room, the monogrammed hand towels and untouched rosebud soaps in the bathroom, the dried flower wreath hanging over the fireplace. Grown-ups lived here, people who knew how to remove wine stains from white button-down dress shirts, people who loosened their ties at the end of the day, watched TV in the den, cooked pot roast, and sent Christmas cards with their names embossed in gold. They not only knew what a 401(k) was, they had one. Or two. Or however many you were supposed to have.

Erika didn't go with the house. Her dyed red hair and clunky shoes made her look like she was still the teenager, disdaining her parents' bourgeois tastes and sneaking in after curfew. She worked long hours for a caterer, booking and overseeing events. She probably didn't have the time or energy to redecorate.

She handed me my drink and stood next to Nick. And then I understood what was happening. "*Nick* is the ex. The one you spent the weekend with. Nick is the ex-boyfriend."

"Ex-husband, actually," Erika said. She crossed her arms. "Though we were only married for a week. I assumed you knew about all that."

I took a large swallow of vodka. These people and their pasts! I felt clammy. I wanted the alcohol to burn my throat, fan out and fill me with warmth. "So you guys were here the whole weekend?"

"We were in Kansas City," Erika said, as if to emphasize that at least that part of the story was true. "Nick left his sunglasses in my car. He just stopped by to pick them up." She made a futile hand gesture. The sunglasses were hardly the point.

Nick spoke up. "You probably won't believe this, Thea, but Erika and I didn't actually—sleep together. Well, we slept, but we didn't, you know."

"It's true," Erika said.

"I believe you," I said, though I either wasn't sure or didn't care. "Can I sit down?"

Erika apologized. She and I sat on the high-backed couch with its neatly folded afghan at one end. Nick sat on the edge of a leather ottoman.

"Erika and I had some, well, I guess you could call it unfinished business," he faltered. He looked at me beseechingly. "If you could just, you know—not say anything to Jules. She'll assume the worst. I mean, obviously."

I nodded, but felt terrible misgivings.

"I've made a lot of mistakes," Nick continued. Erika looked up at the ceiling and sighed. "Sorry, Erika."

"It's okay. You're right. You've made a lot of mistakes, and I was one of them. But now, Thea, Nick's going to do the right thing." She turned to him and he nodded. "Nick's going to propose to Julie."

"What?"

"It's true." Nick flashed his mustachey *aw-shucks* smile. "I want to marry her. But I was worried that there might still be something between me and Erika. Lately when we talked—"

"Thea doesn't care about the details, Nick."

Nick nodded. "I love Jules. I want to be with her. I just didn't want anything unresolved to get in the way. I wanted to be 100 percent certain."

I wanted to say, 100 percent certain? What does that look like? What about all the other girls besides Erika who will come along between your wedding day and your dying day? Probably Julie would say yes, against her better judgment, and who was I to interfere? My heart ached for her. Whether or not Nick and Erika were sexually involved seemed almost irrelevant. They'd spent the weekend together in secret. No matter how pure or impure their motives, they had betrayed her. But things were complicated, I knew. And I was certainly in no position to judge.

I wondered where George was, and if he knew about Nick and his mother. If he remembered them being together, or if he'd been too young.

"So what's happened, Thea?" Erika asked. "Why did you come over?"

I wanted to laugh. The day had started out so innocently. Erika picking up her son, Jimmy and I making the beds and washing dishes, then wrestling on the couch. *You little minx, you wench, you trollop . . .* I winced. And now we were all scattered and wrong, and I had hurt both Eddie and Jimmy, and Amira was probably hunkered down somewhere plotting her next move.

"This guy—this guy called today," I began. "Sort of an old boyfriend." I swallowed the rest of my drink. I hadn't eaten much, and the vodka was hitting fast and hard. I explained how Eddie thought I was going to live with him, maybe even marry him. "It was a colossal misunderstanding. But it's my fault for not clearing it up." I told them about Amira calling Eddie, and Jimmy answering the phone.

"Why would Amira call Eddie?" Erika asked.

"Why do you think? She wants me out of Jimmy's life."

Nick and Erika exchanged a glance. They knew I was right.

"Jimmy will forgive you," Erika said. "When he hears your side of the story, he'll understand."

"If you had seen his face. I lied to him. I neglected to divulge this really crucial piece of information. I should've just hung up on Eddie and gone after Jimmy. That's what I should have done."

"So you screwed up," Erika said. "Who hasn't? You were taken by surprise. But Jimmy cares about you, Thea. Tell him what happened, and take it from there."

"But that's why I'm here, that's why I'm driving all over the place and calling everyone, because I don't know where he went, and he's been gone hours now. If he's with Amira—well." Erika put her arm around me and gave me a squeeze. Nick refilled my drink (with tonic this time) then sat in the easy chair across from us. The two of them speculated, but I wasn't listening. I thought of going back to the house alone, the wind blowing outside. I thought of Jimmy lying in bed next to me, how sometimes he laughed in his sleep, a silent laugh that shook his whole body. He never remembered the joke when he woke up. Danny used to talk in his sleep sometimes. All gibberish. His arched foot stroked my leg in the morning, the few times I stayed with him instead of sneaking back upstairs to my own bed. He wore a diver's watch on one wrist, a macramé bracelet on the other. And Eddie. Those summer days with Emily, swimming in the lake, our Esther Williams routines. We used to walk to the village to flirt with the cute guy who sold us ice-cream cones. She had a crush on him, but he liked me better.

The front door opened, and George walked in.

His band had been practicing at a friend's house down the street. Erika and Nick stopped talking. George looked from one of us to the next. He took a step backward. He was still holding his guitar case. I could see what he was thinking.

No, I tried to signal to him. Don't. Not now.

But he barreled ahead. "You told them, didn't you?"

"George. I didn't say anything."

He put down the guitar. His face was already red and puffy with emotion. He started clutching at his hair.

"What are you talking about?" Erika asked. George ducked his head. "Thea? What's he talking about?"

I wanted to get out of there. I wished I'd brought Josie with me. We could've made a run for it, and just left everything behind. I wouldn't have given it a second thought. Maybe I'm wrong about that, though.

George leaned against the living room wall and slid down to the floor. Above him hung a replica of one of those dark Romantic landscapes, John Constable maybe, roiling sky and brown fields with tiny men on horseback. The gilded frame looked as if it weighed twenty pounds. I figured Erika left it there because she couldn't lift it. Though she could've asked Nick. (Did they really not have sex? Did it matter?) A Matisse poster would better fit her tastes, or that Picasso with the hands holding the bouquet of flowers. I worried that the awful painting would come crashing down on George's head.

Meanwhile Erika was demanding answers. George you're scaring me, what the hell is going on, et cetera. What was she picturing—that he'd been experimenting with drugs? Sex? Worse? She turned to me. "Thea?" Her voice had something in it that made me understand motherhood in a way I hadn't before.

"It's about Vivian." I explained to Erika that George and I had only talked yesterday but I didn't know the whole story yet and of *course* I would've come to her once I knew more details, but then all this other drama had happened, and, well, here we were.

"George," I said. He lifted his head warily, and I put out my hand. He took it, and I pulled him to a standing position. I expected twitching, but his face had gone still. "You have to tell us." He rubbed the snot from his nose with the back of his hand. Then he nodded.

Click. That first domino falling, slow motion, and the tapping of the next one, and the next, and the next.

THAT NIGHT

THE DÉCOR IN ERIKA'S kitchen was a whole other problem: a wallpaper border with roosters on it, a wooden "Kiss the Cook" plaque (Betty Boop in a white dress and chef's hat), a collection of Precious Moments figurines lined up on a shelf. As Phoebe would say, "So much taste, and all of it bad." The clock above the sink featured a black cat with outstretched paw crouched at the top, while a goldfish, attached to the minute hand, made its way around the clock face. The paw and the fish only met when the minute hand reached the 12. The cat spent the next forty-five minutes in an utterly illogical position, paw reaching toward nothing. Neither side of the story—cat, fish—was remotely entertaining.

Erika sat next to George at the kitchen table, Nick and I across from them. A scented candle burned in the middle of the table, doing its best to conjure up apple pie. Erika always had a candle lit. Maybe the house smelled bad. My eye inevitably went to that stupid (yet perhaps existentially accurate) clock. George began his story as the fish made its incremental escape for—what? the hundred and fifty thousandth time? I told myself to focus. But I couldn't look at George. He was so miserable.

"Something bad happened, Mom. The night Jimmy's house burned down."

Erika pushed her glasses up the bridge of her small nose. She leaned forward, her arms folded on the table. "Go on, honey."

"Vivian left her bag on the porch. I ran up and I—I took it. I was just messing around. I thought I could keep her from leaving. I hid it in the barn." George was calm once he started talking. No involuntary movements.

"That's not so awful, George. You were just playing. You weren't stealing it or anything." He gave her a "just wait" look.

"I fell asleep. Then the smell of smoke woke me up. I ran out of the tent. The smoke was coming out of the upstairs windows. I didn't know what to do. The batteries in my walkie-talkie were dead, so I started to run up to the pond." He rubbed his eyes, as if smoke were in them still.

I kept putting my finger in the candle's melted wax, coating my fingertip with a hot white cap, letting it harden, then peeling it off and rolling it into a little ball. I lined up the wax balls on the table and thought of the carpenter bees. Jimmy should be here, I kept thinking. Jimmy should be hearing this, not me.

"But then I thought I saw something. In the bedroom window." He scrunched up his face and shook his head as if to clear the image from his mind.

"What? What was it?"

He took a deep breath. "Vivian."

I jerked my finger away from the candle. Nick covered his mouth. For a split second, George looked almost satisfied. As if we were finally getting it. But then he whispered, "She was trying to escape."

"George—"

"She broke the window with a chair. She had one of those, you know, hard-backed chairs, like for a desk. I heard the glass break. But then there was a lot of smoke and flames, and I couldn't see her anymore."

Erika and I stared at each other. George kept talking.

He told himself he was imagining things, because it was dark and Vivian should've already left. And then he was worried because she didn't have her bag with her and she probably needed it. His plan had failed. She would know he was the one who'd swiped it. They used to play harmless pranks on each other, and he just wanted to play one more. All of these thoughts came fast, he said. One on top of the other. It was all so confusing. He wondered if he was dreaming.

He was caught up in the spell of his tale. "You and Jimmy came running down the hill, remember?" he asked Nick. He nodded. "I think you guys ran to the cistern. And Julie went to the neighbor's house to use their phone, to call for help. Because obviously Jimmy's phone was in the house, burning up with everything else." He rolled his head around as if to get the kinks out of his neck—a thing he sometimes did to preempt a tic. "Amira and I were in the barn. And I told her right away, I said, 'I think Vivian is still in the house. Somebody needs to go get her.'" At this he started crying again.

Erika put her arm around George's shoulder and kissed him hard on the cheek. "Oh, Georgie, I'm so sorry I wasn't there with you."

Nick lit a cigarette even though Erika had a no smoking rule in the house. His hand was shaking. I could only imagine how he felt, how all this had happened while he was on the scene. I took a cigarette from his pack. I needed something to do. Nick got us a saucer to use as an ashtray.

"Amira said, 'Vivian's gone, she left with Pastor Ryan.' 'No,' I said. 'She didn't, I saw her, she's upstairs.' 'But I came down a while ago,' she said, 'and her bag was gone. She put it on the porch, and now it's gone.' I couldn't tell her I took it. I couldn't tell her because then it would all seem like my fault." He put his face down on the table for a moment, but sat right back up. "Then the whole house was on fire, and oh my gosh, it was really loud. I couldn't believe how loud."

Eventually the volunteer firefighters arrived, though too late to save anything. All they could do was prevent the flames from spreading to the fields. Julie was back by then, and she and Jimmy and Nick stood watching the house succumb. Amira and George were still taking shelter in the barn. She had begun to coach him, as if preparing a key witness to take the stand.

George, we'll all get in trouble, if they think anyone was in the house when the fire started. Do you want us to get in trouble? You? Me? Jamie? And she went over the story again, how he had been asleep, how he had woken up and the house was on fire, how he ran up to the barn. *You are a little boy and you imagined Vivian in the house because you were still half asleep and you were afraid. It's okay that you were afraid. You are just a little boy and sometimes you don't understand things. You don't even really understand why Vivian left, do you? Vivian's gone to make a new home with new people, and she'll probably even find a new little boy to be her special buddy like you were her buddy. I'm telling you the real story because if you tell your version of the story, bad things could happen.*

She talked on and on like this, George said, and he was almost sleepy listening to her voice, he almost felt hypnotized, with all the commotion going on around the burning house, which didn't seem quite real, which seemed like another dream or a movie—Jimmy and Julie and Nick running around and yelling and later talking to the firefighters, and he and Amira safe in the barn away from the smoke and the heat, and all the time that duffel bag hidden away in the loft, and how worried he was that Amira or someone else would find it up there and he would get in trouble.

Vivian came up to the pond to say good-bye. She kissed you good night in the tent. You were already asleep, she told us that. 'George is sound asleep. Ryan is here. I'm going now.' She was wearing her Human Bean shirt. She had her hair in a braid. After she left, the fire started. Who knows how? It's an old house. A lot of things could have happened. But we're lucky because nobody, George, nobody got hurt.

Amira was smoking a clove cigarette, and George recalled how terrible it seemed to light a match at that moment, to smoke while the house burned, and how George hated the smell of clove cigarettes because of that night and because of Amira. At first clove cigarettes seemed like such a nice smell, but pretty soon they made you unable to smell anything else, and what had seemed pleasant before made you sick.

Nick and I extinguished our own cigarettes guiltily. I was already sorry about the ash taste in my mouth. Erika took the saucer and dumped the butts. She got a box of tissues and wiped her eyes. She gave a tissue to George. He swiped at his face ineffectually, and I could see her resisting the urge to hold the tissue over his nose and say, "Blow." The goldfish on the clock was about as far away from the cat's paw as it ever got.

"I'm really sorry, Mom," George said.

"I wish you had told me, George. Don't you know I'm on your side? Always, always, always, on your side? From day one, now and forever?"

"I wanted to. I really wanted to. But I was scared. Amira—" He couldn't finish his thought. "Yesterday, Thea came into the barn. And I decided to show her Vivian's bag. I was tired of keeping it secret."

"Dude, I'm so sorry," Nick said. He had one hand on his chest as if to pledge his allegiance, or ease his heartache. "I should've been there for you. I should've protected you."

"It's not your fault," George said. He reached over to pat Nick's forearm. Nick bent down and pressed his forehead to George's hand. George smiled.

Later that night, George continued, Julie took him home to stay with her. "I guess you went home, too," he said to Nick.

"Jimmy and Amira stayed at my place that night."

And then George started having nightmares about Vivian. He kept seeing the chair, the glass breaking, the smoke billowing up. He couldn't have made up that chair. How could he invent such a thing when he knew nothing of fires or being trapped by fire or trying to escape from a house that is on fire?

And one other thing, he said. Something else he kept going over and over in his mind. What Amira said about Vivian's shirt. He knew the shirt she was referring to—the one with the big green string bean on the front. But Vivian wasn't wearing the Human Bean shirt. She was wearing the Grateful Dead shirt. The black one with the big white skull and flowers on it. He could still see it, that skull, disappearing in the smoke.

Afterward, whenever he was around Amira, she was always watching him. It made him nervous. Once she came into his room and sat on his bed and told him that she had received a postcard from Vivian. Amira explained, in a fake cheerful voice, how Vivian was living in the Andes, teaching children in her village how to read. She recited Vivian's message from memory. "'Every day I rise early and work very hard, and at night I sit with all my new friends and we make dinner together like I used to do back home. My life here is filled with many joys. Give my love to everyone. Tell George I'm sorry I haven't written to him, but there are so many children here who need me. I'm sure he'll understand.'"

"Can I see the card?" George had asked.

"Sure," Amira said. "I'll bring it over sometime. But don't say anything to anyone else. They might be jealous."

"Why did she only write to you?" George asked. He felt suspicious then. He didn't want to be mean or rude, but the words left his mouth before he could stop. "Vivian didn't even like you."

Amira jerked her head back. "Why do you say that?"

"It's true. She told me." Only Amira could tell he was lying. She laughed at him.

"No one ever believes a word you say." She leaned down next to him, so that he could see the moles poking out of her chest and smell her stale smoker's breath. "Even your mom. She told me and Vivian that she's worried about you. How you lie about stuff, and how you don't fit in at school. She's worried because everyone, George, everyone thinks you're a freak." And she walked away.

Erika let out a sob. "I never—I never said those things about you." She hugged George again. But there was something in her reaction that suggested maybe she had said it, or something close. If you had a kid like George, I reasoned, and no father on the scene to help carry the burden, you would worry about him. You might talk frankly about him to your friends. You'd still love him. Maybe you'd love him all the more.

Amira never spoke to George about Vivian after that. Or about the fire. "She never talked to me much at all," George said. "And I was glad. I hated her. I hate her now. I hate her so much."

"Oh, honey," Erika moaned. She held him, and he looked at me from over her shoulder, and we smiled sad, reassuring smiles at each other.

~

After George went to bed, the rest of us stayed up for a long time. We felt as if we'd run into something head-on, and now we sat slumped at the table trying to absorb the shock.

Vivian was dead. Jimmy had divorced a dead woman. Amira wanted to keep it quiet and was even willing to terrorize her friend's son over it. Amira, who had practically been Vivian's social worker at one point for God's sake, had been her lifeline—"They were like sisters," Jimmy had said—Amira didn't want anyone to know that Vivian was in the house when it burned down.

And what about Ryan? Where was he in all this? We wondered at first whether he'd died in the fire, too—*if* she really had died in the fire (we kept repeating "if, if, if," though we all believed that George was telling the truth). But if Ryan had disappeared, people would've inquired. Not so for Vivian. She was, in effect, an orphan. Ryan had a church, presumably a following, and people in a Chilean village depending upon him. If he didn't show up, someone would've come around asking questions.

Nick struggled to tell us what he could remember of that night. His memory was foggy, as memories are. Still, George's story made sense to him.

We had so many questions. The crisis with Eddie was minor in comparison. I needed to talk to Jimmy. Erika called Amira's house, but there was no answer. She didn't bother leaving a message on the machine. I called Jimmy's number—"our" number—but no answer there either.

Around eleven I drove home, though I tried to stop thinking about it as home. It was Jimmy's house, always Jimmy's.

I thought of Vivian packing her bags, excited for the next chapter, in love again and full of purpose. I remembered Jimmy telling me about how she used to hitchhike from Topeka to see him. Hitching was routine for her. She'd hitch to Jimmy's and hitch home again. I'd done a lot of things, but I'd never hitchhiked for a boy. I pictured a girl wearing a pair of jeans and a Grateful Dead shirt, striding up the lane to the county road and walking the three miles to the highway. She'd stand casually, no big deal, her thumb out and the other hand in her back pocket. It wouldn't take long for a car to stop. She'd take the first ride, not caring where she went. No Ryan, no Jimmy, no duffel. No forwarding address. A runaway girl again. She knew how to do it, how to walk away without anybody following her or asking questions.

Maybe Amira was right, and George had been dreaming. I still had a visceral memory of a nightmare I had when I was eight years old. A man came into my room and stood by my bed. He looked down at me for a minute or two, then left. I got out of bed and stood on the landing as he descended the stairs. He wore a dark blue suit and a fedora that was too small for his head. I told my parents the next day. I was certain he was real. Nothing they said dissuaded me. They could say over and over that no black-haired man in a blue suit had been in our house that night, but that didn't mean he hadn't come to my room. How do you refute a blue suit, or a small hat? For years I believed the dream was real. Over time I realized the man was a figure who appeared in my dreams from time to time, and that was all. But I can still recall him in precise detail, and the dread I felt, standing at the top of the stairs.

I stood on the deck where the front porch of the old house used to be. I closed my eyes. I felt the night air and listened to the shrill cicadas and knew what it would be like to be that girl, walking away. I stretched out my arms. I saw myself, lifting up over the yard, higher, as high as the trees, flying over the house and across the miles of prairie and highway, over farmhouses and pasture, milo and sorghum and soybean fields—I could identify all the crops now—and cows and horses asleep in their barns. The sound of wind in my ears. The flapping of my clothes in the wind. And the troubling world far below me.

But that chair. But that breaking glass.

That night I slept in the guest room. Coyotes yipped in the woods. Outside my window, an owl made his faint hooting noises all night long. Eli, I thought. Eli has come back.

CHAPTER 14

A WILD STORY

I WOKE UP EARLY. I showered and dressed, then went to the barn to feed Hans and clean out his pen. Usually I sat on a stool and put the nipple of the bottle through the chainlink fence, but this time I brought the stool inside the pen and let myself talk to him and pet him and I didn't worry about rehabilitation and release. His spots had faded and he was looking more adult, though still small. His tail quivered when he saw me, his ears twitched, and we settled into the rhythms of our routine. He didn't care which side of the fence I was on. I hoped I hadn't ruined him. His wound had healed. Bob had decided to let him go soon so he could acclimate to the wild before autumn came. I wanted to free him from the pen, which was confining now that he was bigger, but I feared for his safety. I worried that he would be unable to find a mate. I wondered whether our time with him had hurt or helped. But for the moment, we were in the dim barn, and the early morning was cool, and we were safe.

I climbed up the ladder to the loft and found Vivian's pink duffel. I took it inside the house.

Jimmy had to come home eventually. I was desperate to tell him George's story. Were there family members of Vivian's to be contacted? If not parents then siblings, grandparents, aunts and uncles? What about the authorities? Wouldn't he need to file a report or something? Maybe I'd end up staying another day or two. Maybe I'd stay for another week. I couldn't think past the conversation Jimmy and I would have.

I also needed to deal with work. I was expected at the professor's, and at the bookstore in the afternoon. I called one of Julie's employees to cover for me. Thinking about Julie, and Erika and Nick, was another punch in the gut.

Then I called Dr. Pierson. "I won't be able to come to work today," I told him. "Something has come up."

There was a long pause. I could picture him in his crowded study, knew just how the sun was coming in at that time of morning and how he'd tug at the extra-long string attached to the blinds, lowering them to keep out the light.

"You aren't coming back, are you?"

I hadn't thought I was quitting, but I supposed I was. "It's not because of you. Or the—job. I'm going back east. I've got some unfinished business." I cringed, remembering Nick's use of the same phrase. But when I said it, I knew I had decided. I *was* going back east. "Anyway, I wanted to say I'm sorry. I've behaved badly."

"No, Dorothea. I'm the adult here. I should apologize to you."

"I'm an adult, too," I countered, but in an unfortunate petulant tone. "Old enough to know better, at least."

"All else aside, you've been an outstanding assistant."

I laughed. "Oh yes, outstanding at so many things."

"Don't do that. Don't self-deprecate. It's dishonest."

"Okay."

"No, listen. You know you're smart and capable. When you act as if you aren't, you're doing yourself and others a disservice. You're letting yourself off the hook, taking the easy way out. I see you, Thea. I see more of you than you think." He paused, as if waiting for me to make the obvious joke. I kept quiet. "I'm sorry if I'm speaking out of turn."

"It's fine," I said, though I was stung by his rebuke. "Anything else?"

"I want to reiterate that I'm not proud of how I've behaved," he said. "With you and—well, mostly with you."

"Apology accepted."

"And I'll write you an excellent letter of recommendation. I'll put it in the envelope with your last paycheck. Pick it up before you leave."

"Thanks." He seemed to expect something else from me, but I wasn't sure what else to say. "I hope you get your book done. I hope—I hope you and Mrs. Pierson are happy."

"Ah, Mrs. Pierson. Amanda and I mostly go our separate ways, as I'm sure you observed. Still, she's stood by me." He stopped, thoughtful. "You do know that we were separated at the time of the accident?"

"No, I didn't know."

"Funny, isn't it, how one is willing to be open about one's life with someone who's no longer going to be in it. But yes. She'd moved out. After the accident, she came back to help me get settled. Then six months went by. Then a year, and another. And here we are."

All of this was wildly depressing. "I'm sure you still have good times together."

He talked for a few minutes about their common interests: attending the Kansas City Symphony, watching old movies and college football on TV, playing cribbage on Sunday afternoons. "It's a good enough life, given all the givens. It's probably all we can hope for." He asked me to hold on, and I knew he was rummaging around for paper and a pen. He'd been toying lately with writing a self-help book after publishing the scholarly one, though he knew his colleagues would denounce him for it. One day maybe I'd find his title featured in a bookstore. *Good Enough: All We Can Hope For.*

"So does she know about the . . . maid costume?"

"She knows. She puts up with it, in her way."

"I'm glad you have someone you can depend on."

"And what about you, Dorothea? On whom will you depend?"

He was playing a new part now, the tactful, solicitous employer of his much younger employee. I ran my finger along the rim of the smooth wooden bowl. These days it held a stray poker chip, a miniature troll doll with green hair, a couple of batteries that were either dead or not, a large safety pin, and the usual loose change. Jimmy's keys, too, when he was home.

I started to say, "Myself, as usual," but it seemed flippant, and false. "I'm not sure," I said.

He assured me everything would work out and wished me luck. We said good-bye. Neither of us hung up for a moment, as if we were waiting for something else to happen. Then I heard his familiar sigh and the click of the receiver.

~

Now I was starting to get mad at Jimmy for bolting rather than sticking around and working things out. Or not working them out. I wasn't about to call around looking for him again. I felt certain he was with Amira. I walked around the house. I checked drawers and closets to make sure I hadn't left anything behind. Eddie would tell Emily everything now. I needed to hurry up.

I put Vivian's duffel on the kitchen table. I removed the clothes and the toiletries bag. She and I used the same brand of deodorant, the same pink disposable razors. I tried on one of her T-shirts, and then the jeans with the embroidered rose on the pocket. The jeans fit perfectly. *He always goes for the skinny girls.* I shuddered. I changed back into my own clothes, then tried on the shoes. They fit, too. Not the kind of thing I'd usually wear, red Converse tennis shoes. And they had those fanciful designs on them, silver loops and lines and swirls. I laced up the shoes and propped my feet on the table.

I went through my savings account passbook. I liked depositing money and not checking the balance so I could surprise myself every now and then with the amount I'd accumulated. Like tucking an extra five or ten dollar bill in a winter coat pocket, a gift for my future self. I'd saved a tidy pile over the summer. I squinted, trying to see my next apartment or the bedroom in someone's house I'd rent, but the picture was blank.

I wasn't letting myself think about what it actually meant to leave Kansas. To leave Jimmy. I wasn't sure how I felt. These were my feelings. How could I not know them? I got out the road atlas and checked my hypothetical route. I hypothetically marked it with a highlighter, a long yellow line from here to there, and traced my finger from town to hypothetical town. Columbia, Effingham, Dubois. That old excitement burbled up—something new is going to happen! Then the second-guessing again. Was this really what I was going to do? Leave?

I liked my life here, but . . .

I loved Jimmy, but . . .

I flipped through clothing catalogs and cleaned out the fridge. And then I heard wheels on gravel. I rushed to the window. Jimmy wasn't alone. A car followed his truck. Amira! What was she doing here? Could he do nothing without these people as witnesses? I placed my hands on the counter of the kitchen island to keep them steady. I'd have to wait before I could talk to him. I didn't know how to face her, knowing what I knew. He parked the truck but didn't honk the horn for me the way he usually did.

Amira unloaded a bag of groceries from her car. Of course. She would clip her hair back with the barrette, invite people over, prepare a feast. I watched Jimmy walk toward the house, my heart pounding. He opened the door, dropped his car keys in the wooden bowl. He didn't look angry. Just weary. The dark purplish shadows were still under his eyes. He hadn't shaved or combed his hair.

"Hey," I said.

"Hey." Josie, who'd been fretting all day, trotted over for a scratch behind her ears. "I guess we can talk later?"

"Okay," I said. "But I just want to say that I'm so sorry. I should've told you about—Eddie. I promise you, it's just a misunderstanding. A big fat misunderstanding."

"Yeah, I figured it probably was. Still." Easy come, easy go. He opened the door for Amira and took the grocery bag she was lugging and set it on the counter. If you'd seen that exchange, the opened door, the bag, and you didn't know what was what, you'd assume *they* were the married couple, and you'd wonder who the heck I was. Josie barked a few times then went to the laundry room, knowing I'd put her in there anyway.

"Well, hi there," Amira said, as if she hadn't expected me of all people to show up in her kitchen.

I managed a hello. I couldn't stand her smugness. She thought she had won.

Just wait, I wanted to say.

But looking at Jimmy put me in a different mood. I hated that he'd gone to Amira for solace. He'd no doubt told her about the Eddie fiasco. At the same time, I wanted to protect him from the bombshell that awaited him. I wished I could reach out to him now, touch his arm, hold him. He was just standing there, staring at the floor. He had gone quite pale.

"Thea," he said in a strained voice. "Where did you get those?"

I looked where he was looking. Not at the floor. At my feet. I was still, somehow, stupidly, wearing Vivian's shoes.

Amira stepped around the island to see what Jimmy was referring to. Her face blanched.

"Those are Vivian's," Jimmy said. He had taken a step back, as if I were the dangerous one. "Where did you get them?"

I looked at my feet as if seeing the shoes for the first time. What had I been thinking? "George."

Amira made a sound in her throat, then put her hand there as if to quiet herself.

"George?" Jimmy asked. "What are you talking about?"

"He found Vivian's suitcase—" I scanned the room as if for a clue, some hint about how to get myself out of this predicament. I didn't want the story to come out like this. I especially didn't want Amira there to hear it. "George apparently took it. The night Vivian left."

"He took Vivian's *suitcase*?"

"Her duffel." As if this distinction were the important thing. I gestured in a general way toward the corner of the room where I'd set the bag. Jimmy and Amira looked at it, confounded, then back at me. The three of us formed a triangle. It was them against me. "He hid it in the barn. He's kept it in the hayloft all this time. He says Vivian never looked for it, never took it with her, because—"

"What? Because what?" I hardly recognized Jimmy's voice.

"She never left that night. Vivian was inside the house. When the fire started. George saw her."

Jimmy turned to Amira. "What the hell is she talking about?"

I could see her rallying, the wheels turning, her years of courtroom practice coming into play.

"I have no idea. George was, what, ten years old then? Who knows what he thinks he saw."

"I think he's telling the truth," I said.

She waved her arms, exasperated. "Because you know so much about George, and Jamie, and me, and all of us. You've been around, what, a couple of months?"

"He swears he saw Vivian trying to escape. She threw a chair through the window."

"'He swears he saw her.' He was sleeping, for God's sake. He probably dreamed the whole thing. Remember what a fibber that kid was, back when he used to *talk*?" She laughed shrilly, too forced. She couldn't look at Jimmy. She was keeping her electrified eyes on me. Oh, George talks, I wanted to say. He has lots to say.

"Amira," Jimmy said. "Just tell me what's going on." She laughed again as if she, also, couldn't believe what she was hearing. He repeated her name. He moved toward her, but she stepped back. She looked smaller now, against the wall. A long moment passed, everyone just frozen in place. Wind blew through the trees. Branches tapped at an upstairs window.

I considered how my father would view this scene, the three of us caught in this tableau, and I mentally shifted the blocking, improving the sight lines for an imagined audience. Amira would be costumed in something dark, burgundy or eggplant, instead of the green linen shift she was wearing. You'd need a good tech guy to create a spotlight with a soft, fat beam. Blue gels would add to the mood.

"Are you happy now?" she said to me. "Why did you have to come here in the first place? Why don't you just go back to your doctor where you belong?"

"Doctor?" Jimmy asked.

"Med student," I corrected, then waved my hand—it didn't matter what he was. "Amira went through my stuff. She tracked down Eddie's number and called him."

Jimmy looked from me to Amira and back to me. She didn't deny it. He pointed to the table. "Sit," he said. We did. "Talk," he said to Amira.

She folded her hands in her lap, a composed witness on the stand. Her olive face, with its powerful, large features, its beauty/ugliness, was almost tranquil. She lifted her chin and looked straight at Jimmy. "Vivian," she said, "changed her mind. She wasn't going to leave you after all." Jimmy and I both started. "Surprise, surprise, right? Me too. I was surprised, too."

We sat around that table where we'd spent so many nights playing cards or Scrabble or drinking and eating with friends, but I felt as if we'd been transported somewhere else. We were in the middle of a dark forest. Or dangling in cold space. Or in the kitchen of the old house, charred wood beams above us. I could almost smell the ash. I reached down and untied Vivian's shoelaces, then slipped off her shoes and pushed them farther under the table.

The night of the fire, Amira said, she walked from the pond to the house just after sunset to get more beer. She told Julie she'd check on George, too, which she did. "He was fine. He was asleep in his tent. So I went inside. I thought Vivian had left. You remember, how she put that duffel bag on the porch?" Jimmy nodded. "It'd been sitting there since three that afternoon, like she was a little kid who couldn't wait to go to summer camp. She put it right in everyone's way. We had to practically step over it to leave the house. But no one would touch it. And when I went back to the house, it was gone. I was relieved. Good riddance, I thought." She glanced toward the bag now, as if it were somehow to blame. "But when I went inside, I could hear Vivian in the bedroom, on the phone. She was crying, as usual."

Amira had gone upstairs. Vivian was talking to Ryan. She hung up and told Amira she had decided not to go with him after all. "'I've fucked everything up again, and I don't know how to fix it,' she said. I told her she couldn't change her mind. I told her she couldn't put you through all that. You were tired of her dramatics. Weren't we all? How many times I've regretted the day you met her. I had no idea you'd *marry* her." Jimmy flashed a venomous look.

Amira flinched, but continued the story. She told Vivian to leave, with or without Ryan. But Vivian insisted she was still in love with Jimmy. She accused Amira of interfering with their marriage. Jimmy frowned—whatever Amira was referring to, he didn't remember it that way, or didn't want to. Then Vivian brought up some old business from when Amira had worked with the runaway girls. "I don't even know what it was now. But it pissed me off. And I—I slapped her." She shook her head, as if she, too, found it hard to believe. "The tension had been building for a while. All that shit I took from her. All those favors."

Jimmy reached for my hand, which I took gratefully. At least for the moment, we were together in this. Two sides of the triangle.

"She slapped me back," she continued. "Unbelievable, right? I couldn't believe it. I couldn't believe what was happening." Her voice caught and she lowered her head, chin to chest. We waited for her to continue. The room waited. I looked at Jimmy, let go of his hand and signaled that he should help her somehow.

"Amira," he said gently. "It's okay. Just tell me."

She looked around as if she were trying to remember what we'd been discussing.

"Do you want me to leave?" I asked.

"You can stay, Thea," Jimmy said.

"I was asking Amira."

She lifted her eyes to mine. We stayed like that for what seemed like a full minute.

"I pushed her," she said. But she spoke only to me. "I pushed her pretty hard. Harder than I meant to." Each word was a little box she was opening, to show us both what was inside, revealing the truth to me and to herself at the same time. "She fell. She hit her head on the edge of the dresser."

She paid no attention to Jimmy. It was just me and Amira now.

"She knocked herself out?" I asked.

Amira nodded. "It was an accident. She hit her head. She knocked herself out."

"And then you left."

"I checked her. She was breathing."

"She was okay," I said. "She was still alive."

"Yes."

"There wasn't really anything else you needed to do. Just let her sleep it off."

"So I went back to the pond."

"To join everyone else."

She nodded. "All of this happened such a long time ago."

Jimmy scoffed. "Two years ago, Amira. It happened two years ago."

The spell broke. Amira cleared her throat, almost delicately. A small throat clearing that you'd expect from a third grader, getting ready to repeat a difficult word in the spelling bee. *Can you please use that word in a sentence?* "It feels like longer, doesn't it?" she said.

"Right now it feels like last week."

Where was I two years ago? I thought. Twenty years old. The summer between sophomore and junior year in college. I worked at the camp where I met Stephen Lovejoy, who was the resident sailing instructor. After lights out we'd meet in the dock house. The camp closed down when two kids were diagnosed with meningitis. The counselors—we were eighteen, nineteen, twenty years old, we had no idea what we were doing—had to call the parents. I called mine, too. Stephen needed a ride back to the city. He rode up front with my father while Phoebe sat with me in the back, putting her hand on my forehead every now and then to check for fever. I wasn't sick, but I liked her hand there.

Stephen stayed with us for a few days. When I drove him to the train station, he said he'd call me. "No you won't," I said, and he cocked his head at me. We didn't hug good-bye. Adios, I remember thinking. See you in the funny papers.

"I thought," Amira said to Jimmy now, "once Vivian was finally gone, maybe you and I . . ."

"You were deceiving yourself. I never wanted that."

"You did, for a time." She smiled. I looked down at my lap, avoiding Jimmy's eyes.

"Stop it."

Amira sat back and heaved a sigh that seemed left over from some other conversation. She stood up, found a cigarette in her bag, and lit it. I was impressed that she hadn't smoked till now. "I walked back to the pond. I pretended nothing had happened. The whole scene felt surreal. And there you all were, eating the sandwiches I'd made, drinking the tequila I'd brought. No one even noticed that I'd forgotten the beer." Smoking helped her to collect herself, bring the scattered bits together, like tucking the stuffing back into a cushion.

"And the fire? You said Vivian set it."

"You know she was capable."

"Capable and culpable are two different things."

"Bravo, Jamie."

Jimmy touched his chin with forefinger and thumb and nodded, his mouth partly open, eyes to the ceiling. He did this when he needed to hold his temper, like counting to ten. He dropped his hand and looked at Amira.

"Obviously, Vivian *didn't* set the fire. She couldn't have. So now I'm thinking that maybe you did it. Maybe that's what happened. That way you could get rid of Vivian, and any evidence that you'd hurt her, and accuse her at the same time."

"That's a wild story, Jamie. That's a pretty serious accusation you're making." He asked her straight out. Did she set the fire? Did she? She just kept shaking her head.

"It was an accident," she said again, her resonant voice gone raspy.

"An accident like, you lit a cigarette and dumped kerosene on some newspapers?"

"There was no fire when I walked back to the pond. There was no smoke. Anything could've happened. The house was so old . . ."

Jimmy and I looked at each other. "But once we smelled the smoke, you knew Vivian was still inside the house. You knew she was lying there, unconscious."

"I thought she'd come to. I thought she'd gotten away."

"She tried," I said. Amira startled. "She must've woken up when the fire started." I repeated what I'd told them, about Vivian breaking the window.

Jimmy wiped his hand over his face. "I can't believe this."

Amira mumbled something about how she wasn't to blame.

"You're not to blame? You left her there. You let my house burn down. With my wife inside." He banged his fist on the table. The "wife" felt like a punch, to me. Amira seemed to feel it, too. She hugged herself and ducked her head. "What were you going to say, when Vivian woke up? If there'd been no fire, and we'd all come back to the house and found her there?"

"I didn't plan any of this. This wasn't some master plot. I didn't know Vivian was going to bail on Ryan, or that she'd be in the house when I went down there. And I'd been drinking, we'd all been drinking. Vivian, too. She and I had a fight. I didn't care what happened to her at that moment. I was just angry that she'd screwed everything up again. Here she was, about to leave, and then no—no, that'd be too good to be true."

"But George told you," I said. "He told you what he saw. You convinced him not to say anything. You've known about Vivian all this time."

Jimmy stood up. He turned away, his eyes closed.

"That fire moved so fast," she said. "What good could possibly come of thinking that Vivian might be trapped inside? I knew if I told you, Jamie, you'd be the big hero and try to save her. How would that have helped anyone?"

He put his hand up. *Enough.* He leaned against the island. He was thinking of Vivian, probably. No one deserved to die such a terrible death. And then there was all of his stuff. His childhood memorabilia. His work, years of work.

"Jamie?" Amira pleaded. "I was trying to protect you. Vivian would've wrecked your life. Alive or dead."

He laughed. "You didn't want Vivian to wreck my life? So you did it instead?"

I was suddenly thirsty, as if that suffocating smoke were hanging in the air. I went to the sink. The conversation went around and around. I gave Jimmy and Amira each a glass of water. Jimmy drank his and then looked at the glass as if he didn't know how it had gotten in his hand. I took it from him and gestured toward the chair, and he sat down.

Amira began murmuring to herself. "I never could figure out what happened to that duffel bag. I figured she'd brought it back inside, when she decided not to leave. But I didn't see it in the bedroom. Her other suitcase was there. Her satchel, too—she always called it a satchel. Then we got into that fight, and I forgot about it till later." She looked over at the bag. "That one detail drove me nuts. I kept going over and over that night, walking through the house in my mind, looking for that damned bag. I don't know why it mattered. But the way she'd left it there, on the porch, all day . . ."

"You could be convicted of manslaughter."

Amira drew in a long breath. "Don't lecture me about the law, Jamie. The report from that night says *accidental.* And anyway, there's no evidence." Gruesome thought: anything left of Vivian—bones, teeth—was probably bulldozed with the rest of the debris. "All of this, it's just a lot of crazy talk. The DA wouldn't touch it."

"You really don't get it, do you," Jimmy said.

Amira put out her cigarette and lit another as if she couldn't get through them fast enough. "I get that I could waste a lifetime hanging around here, bringing groceries and cooking and cleaning up after your parties like the faithful wife. Waiting and waiting for you. Don't you see, Jamie? I'm the one who's never left you. Vivian left. She had an affair with that *preacher*, after everything you did for her. And this new girl—this young thing you've been shacking up with all summer—she's, whoops! Engaged! Forgot that minor little detail." She took an angry drag. Then she exhaled the smoke slowly, steadying herself. "But I'm here. I've always been here."

"Yes, Amira. You have always been here." He gave her a level look.

Amira's momentary bravado faded. "Jamie," she pleaded.

"The thing is, you had something on me. And it was always there, hanging between us."

She drew back. "I never would've told anyone. You know that. I've hardly even thought about it."

Oh Lord, now what, I thought. My shoulders and back ached with tension, as if I were willfully holding my body together. Jimmy looked at the ceiling as if for deliverance. Then he looked at me. His face said, I'll tell you later.

He turned back to Amira. "We've known each other forever, haven't we? Since freshman year in college. Yup. We go way, way back. And I trusted you, mostly. I wanted to trust you." She started to protest again. "But there was always a seed of doubt."

"Jamie," she practically whispered. "Look around. I built this house with you." She surveyed the room. "I helped install that sink," she said, pointing. Her voice grew a little louder with each statement. "I stained those baseboards. I screwed in the pulls on those cabinets. I went to an antique store and found the iron headboard for your *bed*. I even paid for it. I wanted to." She massaged her fingers as if they were stiff or cold. "I spent every weekend here, doing everything I could for you, trying to make everything better."

Jimmy nodded—he knew all that, she didn't need to recite her list of deeds.

"We never should've—gotten involved," he said. "I knew how you felt, and so I was even more in the wrong. But I was lonely. I was drinking too much." He was quiet for a moment. I held my breath until he continued. "When the new house was finished, I began to feel hopeful. And I thought you and I could keep the past in the past. You were dating other people, you seemed happier. We'd gotten to this comfortable place. Just old friends. Then I met Thea. I'd never met anyone like her. And I could tell you were having a hard time, but I couldn't deal with it. I kept thinking, Maybe if I just ignore what's going on, eventually it'll all work out. But, Amira—my God—you, you *drugged* her." He stood again, as if only now grasping the significance of her actions. "How *sick* is that?" He turned to me now. His face was almost haggard in the fading light. "I'm so sorry, Thea. I just let it go. I'm always letting shit go. Not anymore."

"Jamie—"

"It's time for you to leave now."

She put out her cigarette then gathered herself up, her dignity, her bag, her car keys. She turned to Jimmy. "Thea will leave you, too." Her voice dropped. "And when she does, I'll be here."

Jimmy took her by the elbow and pulled her toward the door. He was rough enough that she nearly stumbled. "I don't think you understand, Amira. You aren't coming back." He ushered her outside. He shut the door and locked it. The only time I ever saw him use the lock.

I went and stood by him. We watched to see what she would do. She walked slowly to her car. She didn't look back. Dusk had fallen and a front had rolled in, bringing a low mist. We could barely make out her shape as she dissolved into the night.

I held him, not as girlfriend or lover or any of it. He wiped his face. We limped to the living room and sat down. It seemed impossible to get from this segment of time into the next one.

When Jimmy spoke, he didn't look at me. "The thing between me and Amira. It didn't last long. It barely happened."

"I know," I said, though I didn't.

He leaned his head back on the sofa. "I should call the police. I should do something. I can't believe she's responsible—"

"I'm so sorry." I put my head on his shoulder. "I don't know what to say or do. It all feels like my fault somehow."

"Of course it's not your fault. And I shouldn't have kept you in the dark." He made a joke about historians who forget the past. It was lame, but I smiled anyway.

We made tea and sat together on the couch. I told him George's story, and when I was done, I told him mine. I explained how things had evolved between me and Eddie. I considered telling him about the shenanigans at the professor's house, but in the end, I decided to leave that mess alone.

Then he explained the last piece of the puzzle.

When he met Vivian, Amira neglected to tell him she was one of her juvie cases. He thought she was just a friend. Amira told him later that she was protecting Vivian. She didn't want to embarrass her.

"After we slept together, I had this bad feeling. I asked her how old she was. She looked nineteen, twenty. She told me she was seventeen. That was a shock in itself. But I found out she was lying. She was—younger than that." He only discovered her real age when they applied for a marriage license. He felt guilty, ashamed. That was, he believed now, one of the reasons he went through with the marriage.

I didn't ask how old she was. There were no age requirements for marriage in Kansas back then, so no legal ramifications. Still, "child bride" was the phrase that came to mind. Who knows whether or how or why Amira might've used this information against him, but it had felt dangerous.

I put Vivian's shoes back inside the duffel bag and stored the bag in the laundry room for now. Jimmy heated a can of chicken noodle soup for dinner, as if we were coming down with something and couldn't manage anything else. Then we fed Hans. We went upstairs to bed, Josie following, her head down and her tail drooping. I scratched behind her ears and reassured her that she was a good dog, the very best dog in the world, and that everything was okay. Her black lips curled up, but she remained watchful. Jimmy and I slipped under the covers and lay side by side, the lengths of our bodies touching.

"I have to ask, Jimmy. Why did you go to Amira's last night? Why not Rocky's, or—"

"I didn't go to Amira's. I spent the night at the Motel 6. I didn't want to see anyone. I was humiliated. It felt like Vivian and Ryan all over again."

I never meant to hurt you. That's what people say. Who cares? They did hurt you, intentionally or not. I hurt him. I whispered, again, that I was sorry. He nodded. "Amira found me at the coffee shop this morning. She's been skulking around, waiting for the other shoe to drop. All she had to do was ask the right questions and wrestle the story out of me, then act the part of the caring friend."

I wished I had told Jimmy about Eddie at the beginning—that first night we spent together, after dinner with Julie and Nick. It would've been so much easier.

"I bet if I were the last woman on earth, you'd think twice about getting involved with me now," I said.

"Last woman on earth?" Jimmy closed his eyes. "Thea. Sometimes it feels to me like you're the only woman on earth."

And it killed me, to hear him say that.

I fell into a deep sleep. I don't think either of us moved the entire night. In the morning we were in the same position, holding hands. But things were different. We had traveled through something—separately, and together—and ended up in a different place. The dominoes had fallen. I was sad and also not sad. I felt awake.

While we were drinking coffee and eating toast, Nick called. After George's revelations, he tried to get in touch with Amira. He didn't hear back from her all day. So he'd gotten up early this morning and driven to her house. He wanted her side of the story. She didn't answer the doorbell. The door to her house was unlocked. The place was empty except for the furniture—no clothes in the closet, no dishes in the cupboard, no books on the shelves. Amira was gone.

REARVIEW MIRROR

VIVIAN, IT TURNED OUT, had a sister. Jimmy tracked her down in Iowa. Their negligent mother had died in a car wreck, and their father had never been part of their lives. Vivian's sister wasn't surprised by the news or, Jimmy said, particularly upset either. She wasn't interested in meeting Jimmy or talking much about Vivian. Jimmy gave her his lawyer's number—not Amira, of course, but a friend of Rocky's—in case she changed her mind.

"What a piece of work," he said when he got off the phone. "You'd think I was calling to tell her I'd accidentally run over her dog. Or no, there wasn't even that much emotion. I bet she'd at least cry over her dog."

I felt sorry for Vivian. The dead runaway girl. No one even noticed she had disappeared.

Jimmy talked to a detective at the Merdale police department. There was a follow-up interview, but nothing came of it. The insurance adjuster who'd conducted the investigation after the fire was an old friend of Jimmy's grandparents. He knew the house, knew Jimmy, and he'd signed off on the report without much actual investigating. With no evidence, no missing persons report, no suspect, and only a child as witness to the alleged crime, they didn't see any reason to pursue it.

We went over and over the details, patching together the story. Some discrepancies would never be resolved. Whether Vivian was wearing the Grateful Dead shirt or something else, for instance, didn't seem to matter in the end. We see what we want to see, or else the brain invents what it can't recall, filling in the gaps with likely scenarios.

Word spread. People came to the house bringing food (as if someone had died, and I suppose someone had). The focus was on Amira, not Vivian. Everyone had a story. Amira quickly became a demonized version of herself. No question that she was damaged, and even destructive. But I tried to see her as a woman torn by love. She had loved Jimmy. She had loved Vivian, too, and when Jimmy and Vivian ended up together, Amira must've gone a little crazy. And just as she was about to have a chance with Jimmy, Vivian changed her mind about leaving him. Whatever Amira did or didn't do that night, something in her broke. Then I came along, another skinny waif, occupying the house she'd helped to build and furnish right down to that headboard on Jimmy's bed. And occupying the bed, too.

"You're giving her too much credit," Jimmy said.

"I'm not saying she was a good person. But I think she acted out of desperation." Playing the part of the magnanimous bystander was easy, from this vantage point.

Jimmy and I hadn't yet hashed out what would happen next. We allowed the distractions to occupy the space between us. I'm not sure we would have known what to say, anyway.

~

A week after Amira disappeared, Julie proposed a send-off for Vivian. I told Jimmy I could spend the day in town, but he wanted me there. He wanted to spend every minute with me he could. I'd set my departure date for the following day. It felt like I was just hanging around, waiting. There was no point in postponing what now seemed inevitable. I had a debt to pay, and I was determined to finally pay it.

And so we had one last summer party, for Vivian, whose remains lay somewhere beneath the foundation of the house where we gathered. Julie, Nick, Rocky, Sylvia, Erika, George, Wendy, Bob, Lori, Gigi, Jimmy, and me. We put a small table in the middle of the field behind the barn, where the labyrinth had been. People brought buckets of wildflowers and set them around. The cottonwoods provided shade, and the weather was mercifully cooler.

Julie and Nick arrived together. Julie didn't seem to know about Nick and Erika's weekend. She wasn't acting any differently toward either of them. I remembered her telling me that if Nick cheated on her, she'd break up with him once and for all. "I don't have time to go through all that again," she'd said. I recalled her mastectomy scars. I wondered if Nick missed her breasts. If he did, he'd be a cad to admit it. When Erika and I carried some chairs from the house to the field, I started to ask her about George. She assumed I was bringing up the other business. "I can't believe I thought there might still be something between me and Nick. I feel awful about the whole thing."

"These things are hard to figure out," I offered.

"I think I mostly wanted a father for George."

"Nick can be a father figure."

She brightened. "That's exactly what *he* said."

"Don't worry. You'll find someone who will adore you both."

"Easier said than done. George is a lot to take on. So am I." She made a funny face then adjusted her glasses, which had a habit of sliding down the bridge of her nose.

"George is twelve. In six years, you can start a new chapter."

"Ohhh," she moaned. "You're right. He'll go away to college and I'll be old and all alone!"

Julie walked toward us, carrying a shopping bag. "What's all this caterwauling about?"

"George is going to college."

"Already?" Julie joked.

"Julie, my little boy is starting middle school next week. Everything's going by so fast."

"Of course it is," Julie said. She put down the bag and hugged her. "That's just what it does."

"I'm sorry," Erika said, ostensibly apologizing for making a fuss. But I sensed an undercurrent and busied myself with a tablecloth.

"Nothing to be sorry about. Here, help me with this stuff."

She'd brought some photos of Vivian, each in a frame that Nick had made. There were six or seven altogether: snapshots of Vivian and Jimmy sitting on a dock, Vivian mugging with a bunch of other girls, Vivian and a much younger George frosting a cake together, Vivian sitting on a horse and waving at the camera, Vivian laughing, head thrown back, on someone's lap—Amira's? Hard to tell. Then there was a Sears portrait (that ubiquitous blue background) that looked like one of those school pictures they show on the evening news whenever a girl goes missing. Vivian's long, dark blond hair was parted in the middle and styled into corkscrew curls. She had dimples and full lips, shiny with purplish-pink gloss. She'd held the pose a moment too long. Her smile was frozen, her eyes too wide. The picture didn't match the girl I'd heard about. She didn't look like someone with a past. She looked small-town pretty. Uncomplicated.

"Pretty girl," I said. "Not how I'd imagined her though."

Julie picked up the portrait and held it at arm's length. "This doesn't really look like her." She took one last photo out of the bag. "This one is more accurate." A black-and-white 5x7 of Vivian sitting on the grass, folded arms on bent knees, chin resting on a wrist. She seemed unaware of the camera. She was looking up at someone who stood in front of her, out of the frame. There was something pained in her expression, a wistfulness or longing, as if she knew that whatever it was she wanted, she would never get it.

"She was a fierce mess," Julie said, "but also quite loving. She used to take me to my chemo appointments in Topeka. And she did regular battle with this one mean nurse. It became a whole shtick between them." She smiled, remembering.

We displayed the photos on the table along with other Vivian paraphernalia: her blank journal, a shoebox of fossils and arrowheads that she and George had collected, the red shoes. Jimmy had thrown out everything else in the duffel, but I asked to keep the shoes. "If that's not too weird," I'd said. He said it was a little weird but he didn't have any feeling about the shoes, one way or the other. They were just shoes.

We stood in a circle. I was standing between George and Rocky. Jimmy was next to Julie. He kept his eyes down, listening to what everyone had to say.

"I was mad at you for a while, Vivian," Julie began. "The way you left—we thought you left—and never contacted any of us, well, it irked me. We knew you wouldn't stay in touch with Jimmy." She smiled her crooked-tooth smile at him. "But I thought you'd write to George at least. And when we didn't hear from you, I figured you didn't want anything more to do with us. I'm so sorry we didn't try to track you down. I'm sorry for what happened to you."

Then other people spoke. Sylvia described Vivian's crazy dancing, Gigi recalled the time that Vivian asked straight-out what her leg brace was for and "was I born like that or what," George talked about their hiking adventures. He hoped she wasn't mad at him for taking her bag that night.

Jimmy was the last to speak. "Let's be honest. Vivian was a basket case." Everyone laughed. "She and I had some good times, but ultimately we did not succeed in making each other happy. Maybe we were too young, maybe she was too unstable. I don't know. I do know that when she told me about Ryan, I genuinely hoped she'd found what she was looking for." He bowed his head. "May you be at peace, Viv. You deserved better than you got." Viv. I had never heard Jimmy use that nickname before. I don't know why it gave me such a pang. I studied the photo of ringleted Vivian as if she, like the star witness at her own trial, would speak next. But Vivian's story was over.

Bob opened a bottle of Korbel champagne, Vivian's favorite drink, and we filled our plastic cups. The sun had already begun to set along the silver-blue horizon. Every day was a little shorter than the last. Fall would be here soon.

∾

Around seven-thirty that evening, as we were serving steaks and salad and grilled corn on the cob, an Airstream turned into the lane. Wendy and I watched from the deck, trying to figure out who had arrived. Not anyone we'd invited—we were all there. And we weren't the kind of people whose friends drove Airstreams. The thing lurched and swayed along the lane's curves and bumps, stopping before each pothole (and there were many) before carefully proceeding again.

Jimmy joined us. "What the heck?"

We shrugged, intrigued. But the camper got closer, and the situation became clear.

"Oh my God, Thea," Wendy said. "It's your *parents*."

Yes. My parents had arrived. I should've guessed. "How on earth did they find me?"

"They're not as incompetent as they seem."

"This should be interesting." Jimmy smiled.

My father brought the camper to a stop in front of the barn. My mother popped out of the passenger side, jumping down from what looked like a great height, given her stature. The evening sun lit her frizzy hair from behind, like a pink halo. I walked out to greet them.

"There's my girl!" she said. Josie thought Phoebe was talking about her and bounded toward her, which made everyone laugh.

I hadn't seen my parents for almost a year. We embraced, and I felt a surprising welling of emotion. The group on the deck, half-filled paper plates forgotten in the kitchen, applauded. My parents clasped hands and bowed deeply. Whistling and clapping only encouraged them.

"What are you guys doing here, Mom?"

Phoebe looked at me as if I were the crazy one. "I told you we were going to stop by. On our way to California. Don't you remember?"

"It never occurred to me that you'd actually do it." She shoved me playfully. She'd lost Jimmy's number, so she called Wendy. Bob had given her directions, but in his usual spacy way had neglected to let me or Wendy know.

I guided the two of them toward the deck, encouraging everyone to continue serving themselves. I reminded myself briefly of Amira, but in a good way—keeping the party going, urging guests to eat and drink.

Lyman and Phoebe looked older but also glamorous. She was wearing a black T-shirt dress and a string of pearls, as if that were appropriate camper attire. He wore a nautical cap and a pair of Top-Siders to go with his khakis. His closely trimmed beard had some white in it now. I had forgotten how handsome they were, how compelling, how diluted I felt in their presence. And yet I was proud of them, too, pleased to show them off.

Wendy joined us on the deck. I had long since stopped thinking of her as my aunt, or half aunt, or whatever she was, until she hugged Phoebe and they laughed about being related—one so tall and imposing, the other so diminutive. Wendy welcomed Phoebe and Lyman to Kansas with her signature exuberance then left us to admire the view. I pointed out Jimmy's garden and told them that he had built the house, which impressed them. We talked about their trip, their itinerary, Maine.

"So no more vanishing acts?" I asked my father.

He laughed heartily, his gold spectacles glinting. "Dot, your mother is such a flake. She's more of a flake than ever. In fact, I'm getting concerned."

"Oh, Dad, she's always been like this."

"The thing is, I *told* her I was going away for a couple of days. I don't know why she freaked out."

"I can hear you two, you know," my mother said. She was checking out the fields, the light, the sky.

"Did that Eddie person get in touch with you?" Lyman asked.

"He did."

"What a strange boy," Phoebe remarked. "Some letters were forwarded to us in Camden. I opened one—I hope you don't mind. He has quite an imagination."

"He's Emily's brother. That's her car." I pointed to the Buick. But Phoebe was distracted and made a "I just remembered something" gesture. She dashed off to the camper and came back with three or four envelopes, tied up with blue twine. I recognized Emily's handwriting right away.

"You know," Lyman said, stroking his chin, "we could hitch that car to the camper and deliver it for you, after our westward jaunt."

"That's a splendid idea," Phoebe agreed. "It'd be nice to have something to drive around San Francisco. Your dad hasn't thought about how we're going to deal with that *boat* on those narrow streets."

"Thanks, but I need to do this myself. I need to—make amends."

"Oh, amends," Phoebe pooh-poohed. "They're overrated. You're so young, for amends. And it seems so nice here."

We stood together on the deck. The sky looked like egg whites beaten to soft peaks. "It is," I said. "It's really nice here."

We moved into the kitchen for drinks. I tucked Emily's letters inside the canvas bag that held my wallet and other stuff. Also in the bag was the envelope from the professor. I'd stopped by his house after picking up my boxes from Wendy's garage. His good-bye had been remarkably restrained. He shook my hand warmly, but with no leering grin, no suggestive eye twinkle, no salacious last requests. His letter of reference was filled with hyperbolic praise. No one would believe it, though maybe the department letterhead would help. And he'd grossly overpaid me, just as I'd anticipated. *You earned it*, jeered a voice in my head.

My father sidled up next to me. "Add this to the stockpile," he said. "Open it later." He handed me a thick envelope. I figured he'd also written me a check, maybe included a long letter or photos of the old house. I thanked him and kissed him on the cheek.

My mother and I chatted at the table. I felt less impatient with her than I used to. She seemed fragile, vulnerable. She kept touching me lightly, patting my knee or stroking my arm, holding my hand, fussing with my hair. "The haircut is adorable," she said. "Maybe Wendy can do mine." When I told her she looked healthy and fit, she lifted up her dress to show me the progress she'd made on her abdominals. "I do sit-ups while Lyman drives." She was wearing little girl's underwear with ladybugs on them. She often shopped in the children's department. I tugged her dress back down. "That's marvelous, Mom."

Lyman laughed. "She's incorrigible."

Jimmy, who had spoken briefly with my parents outside, joined us at the table. My parents took to him instantly, my mother leaning into me and whispering loudly, "He's quite good-looking, isn't he?" I patted the back of her hand. Jimmy opened another bottle of champagne.

"Here's to the last days of summer," he said. Teaching would start for him again in a couple of weeks. The semester started early there, before Labor Day. He put his arm around me, pulled me in and kissed my cheek. I inhaled his lovely gingery neck.

The beginning of my trip seemed so long ago. I'd almost forgotten about the pie, how I'd decided to eat a piece of pie at every truck stop along the way. But I must've told Jimmy, because he had made apple pie for dessert. He cut me the first piece and served it with a slice of sharp cheddar cheese because he knew that's how I like it. The crust was flaky and rich, and the apples were sweet-tart, not mushy. I finished my slice and held his face and kissed him.

"That," I said, "was the best piece of pie so far."

And then people started coming back into the house, and many conversations were going on at once, and I put down my drink because I wanted to take everything in. Wendy sat with us and beamed, visibly brimming with joy. When Phoebe, Wendy, and I were left at the table—I could hear my father a few feet away, talking to Nick about sailing—Wendy told us her news. She was pregnant.

We congratulated her, my mother clapping gleefully. "Oh, you're about to be transformed," she said. "You are about to be transformed by love."

"Is Bob happy?" I asked.

"He is. He's surprised at how excited he is. Of course, I knew all along he would be."

My mother began to dispense child-rearing tips. Raise kids around people who make music and art, make time for yourself, pay close attention—they grow up fast. "They come to you as they are," she said. "It's 90 percent nature, if you ask me. This one"—she pointed at me, *Exhibit A*—"she was always independent. Headstrong. But I learned to keep out of her way. And look at her now. She's thriving." I didn't bother correcting this revisionist history. On the other hand, she wasn't all wrong.

Wendy and Phoebe babbled about the baby-to-be just like real sisters. I looked around. Nick and Julie were standing together. He had his arm around her, and I knew that he was both a cad and a good person. His heart was loving and flawed, and the flaws couldn't be fixed, and he knew it, maybe even hated himself for it, but in some way he was doing the best he could. And there was George. He had a long way to go yet, but he'd conquered some of his fears. There was a spark of something new in him. Still—middle school. Holy Mother of God. I silently wished him luck.

And then Jimmy. His white-blond hair sticking up a little in the back. He'd been in touch with his dissertation director. He'd floated the idea of finishing his degree. I hoped he would do it. Sometimes the piece of paper *is* important. Of course, I would miss him most of all.

I was sorry to go. I hadn't ever planned on coming here. I had stumbled into this life. And yet, I'd managed to make a home among these people. If I came back, if I stayed, my membership in this clan would become more and more secure. Or else I would be that girl who spent a summer with Jimmy. "Whatever happened to her?" people would ask. I wondered, too.

Before Wendy and Bob left, he and I went out to the barn to see Hans.

"I'll load him into my truck next week, take him far enough away that he won't come back."

I knelt by the pen. "Rehabilitation and release."

"That's the idea."

"Do you think he'll make it?" Hans poked his nose through the fence.

"I sure hope so. He's strong enough, thanks to you. His best chance is now, before it starts getting cold."

"No guarantees, though." I stroked the deer's twitching nose, once.

"No guarantees," Bob agreed.

That night my parents slept in their camper, parked outside the barn. Jimmy and I slept in each other's arms.

"I still can't believe everything," he said. "I'm trying to absorb it all. Vivian. Wendy, pregnant. Your parents. They're a hoot, by the way."

"I know."

"And you . . ."

I hugged him. "Jimmy. I need to finish this one thing. If I don't go tomorrow, I'll never go."

I knew what he was thinking. *That would be just fine with me.* He was quiet for a moment. I almost thought he'd fallen asleep. Then he said, "I don't know whether you're coming back."

I took a deep breath. I tried to see into the future. No list of pros and cons. No Ouija board or crystal ball. I considered making something up to reassure him.

"I don't know either." His head nodded against the pillow. He seemed to accept this. He understood that I was, at least, telling him the truth.

~

My parents were ready to leave for San Francisco early the next morning. "We're returning to the scene of the crime," my mother said. "It's the twenty-fifth anniversary of the first time we clapped eyes on each other." She was nibbling on blackberries, and her fingertips and tongue were purple.

My dad kissed me on the forehead. "Don't worry about a thing, Dot," he said. "We'll get along. Just focus on your own life. If you decide that this is the place, you've found a good man in Jimmy. And if that doesn't feel right, you have other resources to draw on." He reminded me about the packet he'd given me the night before. I found the envelope in my bag and opened it. Instead of the check I'd expected, there was a deed inside, and a map, and photos. Views of the sea. Pine trees, open fields, rocky coastline.

"I bought a nice piece of land in Maine, twenty-two years ago—the week you were born. A nest egg of sorts. It was dirt cheap back then, but it's worth a pretty penny now. You can hang on to it, someday build a house on it. And if ever you need a bucket load of cash, you can sell off a lot or two." He pointed out three lots that could be platted.

I was stunned. I looked at the map. He had placed a gold star on my land, the kind you put on a child's math test. He traced a finger around the property perimeter. "This is where I was, when your mother thought I'd skedaddled. I wanted to walk around the property and imagine you there."

I looked at the deed, the "hereby"s and the "by these present"s. "I can't believe you've kept this a secret all these years."

"Happy graduation, honey." He gave me a long hug.

And now I'd gone from having no place to go to having too many places to go. I could come back to Jimmy. I could sell off some land and use the money to support myself while I explored the possibilities. Apply to grad school, travel, take acting or art classes, manage my own bookstore. I remembered the professor saying, "Thea, you have more options than you're allowing yourself to see." His fortune cookie wisdom turned out to be true.

Jimmy and I waved good-bye from the deck, watching the Airstream lumber up the gravel road, sun flashing off its silver flanks, my mother waving madly out her window as if she were leaning on the railing of the *Queen Mary*. The camper crested the hill and disappeared down the other side.

~

I called Eddie and left a message on his machine, giving him my ETA. I had planned my route down to the mile and would stick to it.

I didn't want to say good-bye to Jimmy. I tried to locate myself in this scene. My life was here, with him. No—my life was elsewhere. No—my life hadn't yet begun.

I promised not to disappear. I promised to call him from the road and let him know I was okay. I watched him in my rearview mirror. He stood on the deck, his blond hair visible even as I turned out of the lane and on to the county road. I already wondered how he would look to me, once he was no longer in my direct line of vision. Parts of the summer would fade quickly. Others would stick with me forever. Jimmy would stick, no matter what happened.

He lifted his hand in a wave. I honked the horn twice.

I cried for several miles, deep chest-sobs that seemed to have been waiting to escape. But by the time I reached Merdale, and the road that led to the interstate, Josie was asleep with her head on my lap, and the emotional storm subsided.

The exits ticked by. The music played on the boom box. I drove for seven hours, making one stop for gas and a bathroom and a quick walk for Josie. I played a game, tricking myself into thinking that everything that had happened was someone else's adventure, or maybe a dream I'd had. The scenes in my mind did have an oneiric quality. I was simply on my way east as planned. Emily was on Yap Island, and I was driving her car to her brother, who didn't think of me as his fiancée but simply as his sister's friend. My childhood home was waiting for me. I'd sit in the backyard drinking sun tea and reading novels, and watching the long shadows fall over the familiar lawn and flowers. All I had to do now was drive, and arrive, and things would work out at the other end.

I pulled off the highway in Terre Haute, Indiana. I found a diner and parked in the shade, in a spot where I could see Josie. I rolled the windows halfway down. The evening had turned cool, and the air felt autumn-crisp. Josie sat in the driver's seat, watching me over the steering wheel. I reminded myself that I had in fact found this dog at a gas station in Grand Island, Nebraska—or she found me. I drove through a storm, and at the end of it, I arrived at Wendy's enchanted house. That was me, doing those things. That was me falling in love with Jimmy, and meeting Nick and George and everyone else, and working for the professor, and thwarting Amira's efforts to sabotage me. It wasn't someone else's story. It was mine.

The diner served an excellent warm mince pie. Probably in the top three, but I'd lost track.

Back in the car, I dug out Emily's letters. I started to open them, then changed my mind. I found a pen and my old astronomy notebook (plenty of blank pages left), then pushed the seat all the way back, propping my feet on the dashboard so I could see my red shoes. A breeze lifted the corners of the pages as I wrote. Josie rested her nose on her paws and sighed contentedly.

Dear Em, I began.

ACKNOWLEDGMENTS

Thanks to Linda Manning for saying yes, and to everyone at Switchgrass Books who made this book possible: Amy Farranto, Nathan Holmes, Pat Yenerich, Yuni Dorr, and Lorraine Propheter. Thanks, too, to Debby Vetter, and to Jenny Wortman for her invaluable editorial suggestions and advice. I began the first draft of this novel during a brief residency at Kimmel Harding Nelson Center for the Arts and am grateful for the time, space, and support.

My love and gratitude to Larry Rodgers for helping me with this book, and with, well, pretty much everything else, too.